The Visiting Professor

Justin Chevet

outskirts
press

Outskirts Press, Inc.
http://www.outskirtspress.com

ISBN: 978-1-9772-2830-7

To Nini, I miss your humorous cynicism and combativeness, offset by your affection, for me, the animals on your farm, and everything French.

To Mrs. Fatimah Sohaila "Sue" Pourreza, growing up, I sadly believed that there would never be a lady like Nini. I was wrong. You are a good mother who loves people and animals and loves to celebrate for no reason, and be passionately combative when arguing. You are a true embodiment of her.

CONTENTS

One

HELPLESSNESS

Helplessness, the powerlessness of knowing a loved one is being sexually assaulted in prison and nothing can be done. Helplessness is the overwhelming despair of hopelessness.

"He was such a good kid!" the mother across the table sobs. "He would never hurt anybody. He is only seventeen! How in Christ can he be in prison?" she asks me.

We are sitting in a windowless but carpeted and well-ventilated room in the Fulton County courthouse, right in the middle of downtown Atlanta. I cannot bear to look them in the face.

"State! What is your recommendation?" asks my colleague, Dave McCullough, who is their attorney. Once a classmate of mine at Atlanta's John Marshall Law School, he is now a father of two, as well as an underpaid but unjustly overworked defense attorney. *I am the state.* I am the assistant district attorney for the state of Georgia prosecuting this case. I am the one personally sending a once promising kid, a freshman at Georgia Tech, to a life of damnation that will include violence, labor, and forced sodomy and sex.

Today, we are doing a plea deal, now required for every serious felony case, as now required by each Fulton County superior court judge, in an effort to lessen their ridiculously massive docket. It is an opportunity to avoid a lengthy discovery process, an even lengthier trial preparation process, and a pointless trial. The plea deal is where the defendant pleads guilty to a charge in exchange for a lesser sentence from the state prosecutor of the assistant district attorney, otherwise known as an ADA. Only a plea deal in this case is pointless, as the Georgia legislature has exacted minimum sentences, thus taking any discretion out of the hands of the bargaining attorneys and the judge himself.

"Well, as you know, Georgia law prevents me from going under fifteen years. That is the statutory minimum."

I know all too well what a young, underdeveloped seventeen-year-old kid endures in prison. In between my multiple tours in Afghanistan and my applying to the only law school to accept me, I worked as a correctional officer in a state correctional facility. It was only a year, but the vivid images that burned into and scarred my psyche oft made me wonder if I was only in law school a year and prison longer.

I know too well what a young seventeen-year-old kid would endure, locked up among the worst criminals. I recall too vividly the massive bodies, and sleek shaved heads, grossly outfitted with loose white jumpsuits. One day I was making my daily rounds. I was walking through the work factory when I encountered a gargantuan man with a tattooed shaved head. His muscular arms bulged from out of his jumpsuit. In front of him on his knees was a young kid who looked to be barely eighteen. He had light features, peach fuzz on his still baby face. The man looked up at the ceiling and loudly groaned as the kid in front of him began to cough and attempt to clear this throat. I broke it up, sending both to confinement.

A bigger inmate would seek out a much younger and much smaller inmate, with lighter bone structure, and offer to be his bodyguard, if that smaller boy allowed the protector to make that kid his woman. The new woman was now compelled to give sexual favors on demand. He was the old lady. He never could leave the side of his protector, and the whole cell block knew that he was a bitch. Occasionally, during my morning shifts, I would see the young eighteen-year-old kid. I could not help but wonder. I could not help but to feel sorry for him. Always there, sitting silently by his protector, as the protector carried on with the other Aryan gang members at the table. Yet, there he was. His tear-stained eyes, staring ahead. It was a sentence enshrined into a more dehumanizing sentence. I imagined how hellish it was to crawl through each day, knowing it would never end. I wondered what this poor kid's life was, before he was a sex slave to this tattooed monster. I could never imagine bedding down every night in that block-bricked-celled sweatbox, knowing that tomorrow it would start all over again. I imagined this poor kid thinking about his life that once was, if he had a job, girl-friend. Now he was here and being slapped around by the force of an animal, for a time indefinite.

Now, today, I imagine this poor Georgia Tech kid, Michael Parent, currently enduring the same godawful manmade hell in Rice Street in the Fulton County jail, nestled along Northside Drive, on the west side of Atlanta, and I am the one cementing his tomb. As an ADA, I feel as though I have once again returned to the state prison system. My time as a correctional officer solidified my dis-dain in humanity. I saw humanity in its truest, rawest form. I always smile when I think of my grandmother saying how humanity is the most disgusting form of life ever to live. Now, I believe her.

Michael had a future. He graduated early from high school and went to Georgia Tech as a double major in electrical engineering and astrological physics. Now, he will be someone's woman for the next few years. He usually kept to himself and studied in his dorm. One night, his friends talked him into attending a party. At first, he resisted but allowed himself to be talked into attending. He en-joyed the drinks and met a young woman, with whom he later had his first sexual encounter.

Unfortunately, the girl was a fifteen-year-old school student who had dolled herself up to gain access to a college party. She bragged about her mighty feat, of shacking up with a college guy, on social media, and the next day, sex crime units were knocking on the door of his dorm.

"He did not know how old she was!" the father pleads.

"Sir, it does not matter in this case. Statutory rape is what the state refers to as a crime of strict liability. Basically, the mens rea, or the intent, does not have to be proven. In other words, sir, knowledge of the criminality and/or intent to commit the crime is completely irrelevant," I recite, as though now it is rote memorized from a script.

"How in the hell is he being accused of statutory rape?" Mr. Parent angrily demands. "He is only seventeen! He is not even an adult!"

"Unfortunately, sir, the age of consent for sex is sixteen, and anyone older than sixteen who engages in any sexual act with anyone under that age can legally be charged with statutory rape, regardless of whether the suspect is a minor or not!"

"He is not even legally allowed to join the army, vote, or watch porn!" his father screams at me.

Ahh, but the morbid irony. He is legally too young to watch pornography but legally compelled to participate in some of the vilest pornographic acts, and completely against his will. The father begins to break down in tears. "I remember only last year waking him up for track practice. He would be peacefully sleeping in his bed, with the cat next to him. The cat's paws would be resting on his back. Now my most recent memory of him is him sobbing and begging me to help, as some burly guard drags him away."

I used to know the father. Never did I ever think I would see him in this state. As a career wrestling coach, he was the personal embodiment of indestructibility. Now he epitomizes helplessness, as he sobs, describing his son, begging him to help him out of a manmade hell.

I watch the mother sob uncontrollably. One mistake cost her son his life. He will spend more than a decade behind bars. When he gets out, assuming he makes it, he will never be employable. He will have no marketable job skills. He will be lucky if he gets to live with his mother in his mid thirties, but most likely will have to live under a bridge that will not fall within a three-mile radius of any school or park.

Helplessness. Whenever I hear the term, I always think of the Benoit and Bourgeois families in France.

Loire Valley, France, 1940

To Anne Sophie, it seemed like an eternity since the Germans took over her city, even though it had only been three years. Before 1940, her life had been so simple. So simple, that she had taken it for granted. Yesterday's perceived crises were now today's fond memories. Now, since the Germans had begun running her city, she wondered if she had even understood the meaning of the word *hardship*. She certainly knew that she had never understood helplessness.

She awoke every morning and made her way to school. She then spent most of the evenings helping her father in his picture frame shop a few blocks up from the city square. Anso, as her friends had oft called her, strategized hard for her free time because there was so little of it. When she was able to finagle some free time, it was spent on the farm of her best friend, Genevieve Benoit, whose father had a spacious farm, overlooking the city.

Anso lived with her family in an apartment, in a centuries-old building, on a cobblestone street, in the heart of the small city. Nevertheless, she enjoyed visiting Genevieve and her family. She would always greet Mademoiselle Benoit as she helped with Genevieve's younger sister Adrienne, who was mentally handicapped. Anso likewise had a special needs sibling, her brother, Thomas, who had cerebral palsy and could not walk.

Anso loved the animals, the space, the beautiful landscape, and sitting upon the hill overlooking the clustered downtown area, where she lived. Genevieve was tough, like Anso. Both girls enjoyed the outdoors; both were abrasive, stubborn, and rebellious. Both girls acted as protectors for their group of girlfriends against uncanny boys, or even adults who may have upset any of their friends.

The afternoon in 1940, before an eternal darkness would overtake her city, and then her life, had been relatively uneventful.

It was their last year. Upon completion of the short summer session, which would end in July just before Bastille Day, she would be done with school and would joyfully embark on what undoubtedly be her blissful adult life. She sat and listened to her effeminate math professor, Monsieur Brunrot, and exchanged mocking glances with her friends.

Their group consisted of Anso and Genevieve Benoit, the tough girls. Chantelle Etienne was the brainy one and well reputed for her intellect, but introverted and shy. Josephine Bourgeois was the pretty one, for whose attention every boy, and many adult men, clamored. She was also the daughter of Monsieur Bourgeois, the mayor of the city. Her boyfriend, Laurent, was a young twenty-one-year-old, whose family was from Toulon, a Mediterranean coastal city on the southern tip of the country, closer to the Italian border.

Laurent did not share the same bodily features as those from the northern and middle provinces of France, who appeared almost British as compared to Laurent, who possessed a tall, somewhat lanky frame, as contrasted with the shorter, portly men in his newly adopted city. He also had dark, striking facial features, rendering every woman envious of Josephine. Josephine's family also had a beautiful house, encompassed by a farm, overlooking the city, not too far from where Genevieve lived. Yet because the mayor as always entertaining guests, Anso rarely got to visit. They could not wait for class to end for the day so they could spend the hour smoking by the river before Josephine had to be at the mayor's office and Anso had to be at her father's frame shop.

After what seemed like all day, Monsieur Brunrot, in his gentle manner and soft voice, dismissed the class, almost begging them to complete their homework, in a manner unlike most teachers of that time, who could be nearly iron fisted.

As the end of the school day approached, even in its agonizing, tortuous, slow passage, the girls could not wait to sprint out of the schoolhouse that was set in the centuries-old medieval building. They spent their routine afternoon smoking by the river that ran through their town and talking about the boys and teachers in their school.

Anso would go stand at the edge of the river and watch the water run while the other girls sat at a nearby picnic table, fumbled about their purses for cigarettes. Anso looked over to see the little beagle dog that always hung around the city park, waiting for scraps that the citizens would feed him. She came to love that animal and often referred to him as her own. She had even given her little pet a name. She called him Minou, or "little one." She reached into her pockets to extract a small piece of baguette she had saved from dinner the other evening. She crouched down next to the river and gently motioned for the dog to come over. She slowly held out the bread and eagerly eyed the dog as he hesitantly moved his little paws to take two frightened steps toward her. She began to feel hopeful that the dog would trust her; he stopped abruptly, spun around, and sped off. Just as the dog disappeared from sight, the girls called her over.

"Anso, quit hanging out by the river! Quit being antisocial and come join us!" Josephine invited as she awkwardly lit her cigarette.

"I swear he is gay!" Chantelle said as she took a long drag off of her cigarette.

"So what if he is?" Genevieve replied, with Anso nodding in approval.

"I don't know. Should someone who is that clearly gay be a teacher, in front of kids?"

"We are not kids!" Anso protested. "We will be done with school this year! I am already an adult! I help with my brother, help my father's shop!"

"I promise you! Brunrot is not gay! I know this!" Josephine interrupted; she stared off over the bank of the river, followed by a long drag off of her cigarette.

"Who is not gay?" an intrusive but all too familiar voice interrupted.

Jean Luc took a long drag off of his cigarette as he approached the unsuspecting girls.

"You know it is not good to gossip!" he said as he moved toward Josephine's face in a mock attempt to kiss her. Josephine quickly moved her face away and hopped down off the table as Jean then thrust his hand toward her purse.

Jean Luc was raised by a single mother, which was unheard of then. After he turned fifteen, his mother could no longer control him, nor could many of the men in the city, and so he terrorized other adolescents at will and relentlessly harassed Josephine. Jean took complete advantage of Laurent's fear of him.

Josephine then yanked her purse away, backing up, as Jean continued to move toward her.

"I can't get a mint?" Jean asked, as he moved closer toward her.

"No matter how much your breath may stink, no, you cannot have anything in her purse! So, leave her alone!" Genevieve demanded as she stood between the two of them, the protector of the group, the tough farm girl. Enraged, Jean stepped toward her, narrowing the space between them.

"What did you say to me?" Jean demanded as he quickly stepped up into Genevieve, enraged that a girl would try to confront him.

Genevieve simply stood there, doing her best to summon all of her courage. Nevertheless, her attempts were visibly failing, as Luc, as well as the rest of the girls, as Genevieve began to shake, complementing her wide, alert eyes.

"I asked if you had something to say to me! Or perhaps are you just dumb like your sister?"

Genevieve's face was flush with anger, but her quivering and tearing face betrayed a fear and hesitancy.

"Ahhh, voila! Good! Then perhaps you are not as retarded as your sis..."

Before he could finish, Genevieve's fearful situation was explosively interrupted by the sound of smacking flesh and disturbing shock as the sight of Jean reeling backward disoriented her. While all the girls realized Anso was bold, Genevieve could not fathom the insanity of coming right up beside someone as towering as Jean and coldcocking him from the side. Genevieve could barely feel her stomach as now she was even more frightened at what was surely coming to her friend. She would have to jump in and help her against Jean, returning the favor her friend rendered onto her, even if unrequested.

"Mention either of our siblings again, and you will know what it is like to be handicapped yourself!" Anso swore as she stood over him. Furious, and crazed with adrenaline, he angrily jumped to his feet, ready to strike, when the sound of a car engine stopped everyone in their tracks, as a patrol car pulled up. The gendarmerie, French law enforcement, stepped out of the driver seat, followed by the mayor, emerging out of the backseat.

"Ca suffit! It is enough!" commanded the mayor. Jean did not have time to hear it, as he was already gone before the gendarmerie could be out of his car.

"Josephine, I expected you at the office half an hour ago! Allez!! And, Anso, I am sure your father is waiting for you at the frame shop; you can ride with us to town!" The mayor then addressed the other girls: "You know, all you ladies will be adults when this school year ends. You will have households of your own to conduct. You will then have no time to sit by the river, smoke, and gossip! You will have adult responsibilities."

"When this year ends"—ah, but how wrong the mayor was.

Anso knew there would be trouble resulting from hitting Jean Luc, and the dread rendered her despondent at the frame shop. But that otherwise uneventful afternoon would produce something much more worrisome, and fearful.

At 5 pm that day, one hour after she had hit Jean Luc, Anso detected a commotion within the city. Both Anso and her father, Monsieur Chevalier, stepped outside to see people scurrying about. German soldiers individually were pushing pleading citizens back into their homes. A handful of German soldiers, cloaked under their burly gray coats, which nearly concealed their faces, as their massive black helmets came down over their eyes, quickly paced down the city streets, their angled and perfectly aligned rifles strapped to their broad shoulders. They shouted commands in a harsh German accent. Roughly a mile behind them were columns of marching soldiers, prepared to lock down her city.

During the past year, as Anso sat in school, counting the days until its end, she had grown aware of news that the Germans were invading many parts of Europe. As a young girl, the snippets of

German aggression she heard on the radio, as her parents would sit next to it, were too far outside of her little world that took place in the city and among her friends. Occasionally, upon visiting the tabac, the small shops in France where French people purchased cigarettes, newspapers, and coffee, Anso would see a local resident hurriedly purchasing a pack of cigarettes and a paper, only to glance big, bold headlines, proclaiming Prime Minister Petain signing an armistice agreement with the German Nazis.

"Petain la putain!" a disgruntled old Frenchman exclaimed under a gruff voice, hampered by years of moderate smoking. *Putain* was the French world for "whore" and became an adequate description for those who believed Petain failed to resist with hardly sufficient vigor.

For years throughout young Anso's adolescence, it was no secret that Germany was on the march. However, Germany's aggression was never her problem, nor did it ever seem to affect her little world that took place in school, in the square, and especially within the protective element of the peaceful sanctuary that was the Benoit farm. Germany would swallow up what was then Czechoslovakia, and Anso was going on her first date. Earlier this year, Germany swiftly and brutally invaded Poland, but Anso was focused on her exams and what she would do with her friends later.

Then in late spring of 1940, Germany rolled through the forbidden Maginot line, in aggressive and symbolic defiance of the Treaty of Versailles, the treaty that ended World War I, that assigned blame on the shoulders of Germany, plunging them into hopeless depression. Two weeks later, Germany rolled through Paris, and Petain had to agree to any terms Germany demanded. Petain signed an armistice, giving the Nazis all of northern and central France from the Atlantic to the German and Swiss borders. The Italians, Germany's axis partners, enjoyed the privilege of occupying the southeast, and because Petain was so cooperative, he got to retain the southwestern region, under what was the Vichy government.

Anso's father tried to usher his daughter back into the safety of what had been their family shop for years. Yet no sooner had

Monsieur Chevalier gotten them both inside and they were followed by a tall, imposing figure, who forced open their door.

"You two!" he commanded in a rough accent. "Lock up your store and return at once to your home! Your business is closed for the evening!"

The soldier had barely waited for them to obtain their personal items and secure the shop before he physically escorted them out of the shop and rushed them down the street, along with other frightened citizens. Anso was too scared to look anywhere except for straight ahead but could see out of the corner of her eye citizens pleading with these seemingly towering, almost inhuman figures, as they listened unpassionately to these now helpless people. Helplessness.

She continued to see barbwire fences erected to surround her city. She had never noticed just how small the city was, as she traveled freely among the outskirts. Now that her city was closed in and cordoned off, she realized how small her world was. She saw a barbwire fence across the river, where she just was only hours prior. A German soldier was pacing back and forth, smoking a cigarette, his rifle slung diagonally across his back.

When Anso and her father had finally entered their apartment, after what seemed an eternal, supervised march, she was too scared to even peep out of her window. When she mustered the courage to do so, she saw her once beloved, narrow, cobblestone streets lined wall to wall with the seemingly robotic figures, their rifles slung across their back, in the same fashion, dissecting their bodies, nearly symmetrically.

They were followed by a row of long, shiny, black, open-top sedans, whose hoods had a small swastika flag on each side, and the side of each car was draped with a huge swastika banner that covered half the car. As frightened as she was, Anso marveled at how pristine and clean each car seemed. Its exterior was perfectly polished; the Nazi banners had not even a piece of lint on them. The last car in the procession had a German officer standing up in the backseat. His uniform was a dress uniform, also impeccably maintained, and his chest was adorned with medals and awards, his arm showing a swastika band. Only the bottom of his dry, pale face showed, as the rim of his polished garrison cap came down over half of his face. Anso could still tell that he was carefully observing the small city he was about to occupy.

Behind the cars were more citizens being rushed into town. Then to her surprise and horror, Anso saw the Bourgeois family being herded down the street.

"I thought they wanted us all indoors?" she inquired to no one in particular. Then it dawned on her.

The Germans were confiscating all the big houses with expansive properties as quarters for their officer, and additional offices. She watched as Genevieve helped her sister Adrienne into Chantelle's apartment, where two families would now coexist in cramped conditions. Then Anso heard a knock on her door. Morbid curiosity overtook her fear of peeking out of her window at the nightmare that would become her life. She saw a once proud, popular mayor standing helpless, frantic, and scared at her door, with his daughter, the envy of the city. The popular Bourgeois family was forced to abandon their chateau that overlooked the city they ran with leisure and efficiency, to beg the Chevaliers to allow them refuge.

Anso had learned from their new guest, the mayor, that many city officials knew that today was coming; they simply didn't want to alarm the people as to the inevitable, for fear of unrest or any other mass action that may provoke the unbeatable force penetrating their city. Outside a loudspeaker drowned out all the other voices chattering in the tumultuous commotion that had once been their orderly, peaceful city.

"Be advised! There will be a meeting in the town square, at twenty hundred hours! Attendance is mandatory! Soldiers will be patrolling the streets and checking store and homes. The punishment for those not in attendance will be swift and severe!" the high pitch, constant laden accent warned in high decibel volume that pitched through the narrow alley ways and blasted through the old stone walls of the medieval city.

That evening, a throng of exhausted and mentally defeated city residents crowded around the city church. Most old European cities, those that had spanned hundreds of years, were designed around the church. European society throughout the Middle Ages centered around the Catholic Church; thus, every European city centered their activities around the church. These were not plain churches but cathedrals, so unlike the plain, boring, quickly constructed churches seen in the United States, unlike those churches seen in a land founded by Protestants, disgusted by the excessive extravagances of the Catholic Church and thus chased out of their own countries for stating such.

How ironic that the leader, Martin Luther, who acted out of such an outlash against the Catholic Church, was from Germany. Across from the church in most European squares was also a grand decorative building that acted as their city hall, or hotel de ville, literally, "hotel of the city." This was where all administrative tasks were conducted, and also the location of the mayor's office. Anso used to always marvel at the magnificent, centuries-old building. She would always wonder what took place in that very building during the reign of Napoleon or the Bourbon kings before him. She was always overwhelmed at the history and human activity to which those buildings were privy.

Tonight, though, she could not stand to look across the square from the church. That wonderful historical building was now draped with a large, red-and-black, imposing swastika banner that covered half of it, in addition to the various swastika flags protruding from the roof. In front of the hotel de ville was a shamed, and tearful, Mayor Bourgeois.

Compelled to look at the deck in front of the entrance to the cathedral, Anso saw three of the thuggish gray coats holding their rifles, standing on the bottom step, staring out into the crowd, ready to shoot anyone who wished to disturb or act out.

On the deck, which acted as a mini stage, approached the same well-dressed German officer Anso saw standing in the back of the vehicle. Although it had been hours since she had seen him, he still looked as though he was recently assembled. His uniform was perfectly arranged, and his posture lent even more dignity to his demeanor. He walked to the edge of the patio and stood there, relaxed, with his arms planted behind his back.

The crowd fell silent at his mere presence.

"Ladies and gentlemen, my name is Sturmbannfuhrer Heinrich Engel, of the German Wehrmacht...or I think it is Major Engel, to point out the equivalent in"—he briefly paused—"well, the equivalent in *your* military," he superciliously corrected as he smiled. "I will be the officer in charge of this city, and my sturm will be running day-to-day operations during this unfortunate period of war. You should be advised that I am in command, as pursuant to the peace agreement endorsed by your prime minister Petain. We are here at the permission of your government!" Major Engel lectured.

"Here standing over to my side, is my second in command, Hauptman Strobel."

Hauptman was the French and British equivalent of captain. Strobel did not look as sharp as his boss, and he did not share the same pale, steely, blue-eyed complexion as the black-booted soldiers who surrounded the crowd. Strobel had black hair and even darker eyes to contrast his pale, almost sickly skin, was short and bulky, and diabolically smiled, as he glared out of the top corners of his eyes.

"We are here in an effort to advance our war effort against Allied aggressors!" Engel continued. "For such a reason, I am afraid, I must use your city to its maximum potential and demand full co-operation and obedience at all times. I further regret that I must impose some austere measures on your city, as we are in a time of war. I will insist that each one of you relinquish any and all firearms and accompanying ammunition that you may possess. This is serious, and I must warn you that should one of my soldiers find even one round of ammunition, even without an accompanying fire piece, the household in possession of such contraband will be imprisoned, for a time indefinite."

At this point, he was done pacing in his crisp but relaxed manner, and he now stood at the edge of the steps, just above the grimacing soldiers guarding him, his stance rigid, his hands relaxed behind his back; his cold, emotionless blue eyes pierced the now frightened and helpless crowd from just under his black, shiny rim.

"I will also insist that all telephones be confiscated, and only German officials will use telephone lines. Communication with the outside will be monitored by German forces, as will travel outside the city. Understand that train stations are to be employed by German forces only, and travel outside the city will be approved only by me or Captain Strobel. Finally, nobody will be out of their homes after eleven at night. After eleven, we will have blackout operations, and should my soldiers see anybody wondering about at this point... they will be shot on sight and with no accompanying questions. I do apologize for these"—he cleared his throat—"inconveniences.

"However, you must understand that times of war require austere measures. With Godspeed, this will end soon, and you may regain some of your conveniences." With that he cracked a meager and forced smile.

Conveniences! Their very liberties of day-to-day life had now been choked to death, and the Major simply saw them as conveniences.

As Anso slowly made her way back to her home, she could not help but be impressed at how quickly the chain-length fences were erected. Only a few hours had passed between when she punched Jean Luc at the river and when she was being shuttled out of the shop, and within that time, the Germans had already locked down her city and surrounded it with fence and barbwire.

Now, Germans were knocking on doors, demanding to inspect private residences for forbidden literature or any sign of decorations or literature indicating Judaism. Windows were being painted black, and street lighting was being cut, so that by eleven that evening, the once beautifully well-lit, old city would become pitch-black, save for the shadowy figures of roving German soldiers and outlines of fences that now locked in their city.

After so many weeks, Anso figured that she would become

accustomed to life under occupation. Life, however, was still a struggle. As much as she loved Josephine and the Bourgeois family, spaces were cramped. Anso took for granted that she could stroll into a tabac and buy cigarettes or go for a coffee at one of the various cafés that lined the old, narrow streets. She took for granted that her family could go buy daily fresh pastries at Mademoiselle Cohen's boulangerie or go buy choice meat at Monsieur Marceau's boucherie. Now everything went to the Germans. The best products were sent to the Strom Troopers, or SS soldiers, fighting the British on the front line. The Wehrmacht, who occupied the European cities, were the next priorities, with the local citizens getting whatever scraps were leftover.

Cigarettes, good meat, and good wine became a commodity, and a people who loved to indulge in these products now found themselves scrounging for and hording any piece of these once ignored items. Businesses closed as their inventory, and profits, dropped substantially, and suddenly cigarettes and wine became currencies in their own right. While the high command required that occupying forces adequately compensate those businesses they patronized, this sometimes did not happen, and the proprietors were often too intimated to say anything.

The last week of classes continued, and the once semi-abrasive, forceful teachers were now soft-spoken and beaten into a surreal timidity. Monsieur Brunrot barely spoke and said as little as possible when demonstrating math problems. Anso, who once hated her teachers, now felt sympathy for them. How frightened they must have been of saying or teaching the wrong way or muttering something that may upset the Gestapo.

Before the occupation, Anso would briskly and cheerily head down the street to her shop, which was miraculously doing all right. She would pass restaurants where once she would see familiar people having lunch now filled with pressed uniforms, swastika armbands, smoking and drinking beer, with a ramrod perfect posture and impeccable manners. She turned the corner and saw a poster warning about Jews and Communists. One poster displayed a fat miser in a tuxedo with a shiny timepiece hanging from his tie. The miser had a long, crooked nose on which rested a monocle. The miser was holding an emaciated child dressed in rags, clearly undernourished and clearly impoverished. The other hand was holding out a wrinkled hand in front of a grim reaper and a devil, who were both standing before him. The miser was holding out his hand as if to demand money. On the miser's ugly, wrinkled forehead was a star of David.

"Ne Laissez les Juifs vendent votre enfants!" "Do not permit the Jews to sell your children," the poster read in large, red letters.

It was difficult for Anso to conceive that those same soldiers, who carried themselves with such grace, carried out every action, to include the way they handled their cigarettes, with such class and impeccable manners, could be capable of such madness.

Anso was reorganizing her inventory when Josephine rushed through the door.

"Salut!" Anso greeted cheerily. In these hideous times, she had realized how much she had taken her friends for granted.

"Salut," Josephine responded, sounding depressed.

"I suppose things are not going so well at the office!" Anso quipped.

"I am glad this is funny to you!"

Monsieur Bourgeois remained the mayor in his own right, but the city knew that he was no more than a messenger for the harsh orders of Major Engel and that Bourgeois had to relinquish his office over to the major, and the hideous Captain Strobel.

"Jo, this is not funny, but you have to find humor somewhere, or you will go crazy!"

"Humor!? Are you mad, Anso?"

"Yes, I know, Jo! It is terrible, isn't it? Being subject to the cruel whims of another is the worst thing. But you just have to keep your head down and not think about it!" Anso replied, still adjusting her inventory.

"I can't bring myself to do it!" Josephine replied in a terse voice.

"Of course! You are the city's girl, the pretty one! Your family always ran the city and commanded the respect of all the lowly people like us!" As soon as she fired that accusation, she instantly regretted it and wished she could withdrawal her condemnation of her friend's character.

However, when she saw her friend frozen in her tracks, her mouth agape in shock, Anso regretted her quick tongue that much more.

"Look, I did not mean…" But it was too late.

"You know, Anso, many guys at school found you much more attractive. They hated your attitude, your cynicism, your dark way of looking at everything."

"Says the girl who comes in here and complains every day. As if the rest of us are just having a wonderful time, shuffling just to keep our doors open and save our businesses from plunging! I guess the great Bourgeois family is no longer in charge, so thus comes the end of the world!"

She heard Josephine begin to sob. She had once again been too hard on her friend in one of many epic rants.

"Anso, the major wants my dad to provide him the names of all Jewish, Gypsies, and reputed Communists and Communist sympathizers! And my father is doing it!" she sobbed.

"Maybe it is just to keep an eye on those he distrusts! Look, Major Engle strikes me as being fairly methodical."

"Methodical? Anso! You really do live in your own world! I guess while I live within the protective confines of the Bourgeois estate, you refuse to look beyond your little world of animals and plants at Genevieve's farm!"

Ah, how Anso wished that were true! She briefly imagined a world composed only of the Benoit farm, the animals, and Adrienne, who would come to spend time with them. Helplessness. One takes their freedom for granted until it is snatched from them. She realized how much she took her friend's farm for granted until now that it was gone. Did we really have to lose something before we appreciated it?

"Anso, the Germans are imprisoning these people! Wake up!" Josephine stormed out of the shop.

Later that morning, Anso was in the back room when she heard the door open.

"Hello!" she called from the back room. She knew most of her father's customers, as the same downtown people would visit their shop, so thought it odd, that only silence followed her greeting.

She rushed out into the merchandise lobby to see one of the German soldiers calmly pacing about, inspecting the different frames.

At first, Anso simply stood in silence, as he had not noticed her there. She watched him study the different frames, his eyes darting from one to the other, comparing and contrasting. Anso herself was studying the soldier, his straight, gray coat and the immaculately mirror-shined boots and equally impressively shined garrison cap. She listened to those boots tap the floor. Then he spun around, and his eyes lit up in surprise. He looked over Anso but quickly regained his nearly robotic composure.

"Bonjour, mademoiselle! I am here on behalf of the city's kommandant, Major Engel. I need a six-by-four-foot solid frame!"

"Mon Dieu! We do not carry such a frame! I mean, my father would have to assemble one!"

"Very well! Then when can I expect it?" Anso felt the rage within her well up. "Oh, and because this is for the commander of the city, it is to be written off as, ahem, contribution to the effort."

Anso was enraged. She had had enough. Never a patient individual, she had more than exceeded her limit of tolerance. She hated the Germans. As one who hated any disruption, no matter how slight, she was aghast at the limitations and constraints that these boisterous boys, hiding behind the façade of gentlemanly officership, had imposed upon the simple life she loved so much. Her eyes narrowed, and she stepped closer to the soldier, ready to enact the venom that made her infamous throughout the city.

Just then, Josephine bursts through the door.

"Anso! Quickly come! The Germans are arresting Monsiuer Brunrot!"

Anso rushed to the door, nearly forgetting about the German

standing in her shop. She quickly rushed back and demanded that he leave, as she was closing the shop, as the soldier stood there dumbfounded.

Anso then followed Josephine down the narrow streets now crowded shoulder to shoulder with citizens rushing to the school building.

Anso and Josephine were barely a few blocks from the entrance of the school. Now, throngs of onlookers blocked the stairs to the entrance, where the girls once trotted up unimpeded, wishing for any obstruction or even excuse to avoid those dreaded doors, now in the most morbid irony, could not get even close to the doors they so wished to penetrate. Two Wehrmacht soldiers were escorting a visibly frightened Monsieur Brunrot down those stairs, to the howling pleas of his mother and sister, who continued to cry, "Si vous plait!" in a futile attempt to appeal to the seemingly nonexistent Wehrmacht sympathies. Next to the school, a German soldier in a dress uniform, with his bright swastika armband, was speaking into a megaphone, his message blaring out among the awestricken crowd.

"This man is a homosexual! Understand that such an obscene, deviant, bestial manner of life will not be tolerated in the new Europe we are forging. This manner of gross activity is an affront to good common decency and acts as an aberration to our moral family structure. Understand that any such activity or those who engage in such activity will be found and will be removed!"

The vocal propaganda continued but was faded out, as many of the citizens looked on with horror as Brunrot was led onto a truck. Anso could see tears streaming down his pale, stricken face, as he was too frightened to utter a sound. She then watched the big metal gates of the truck slam shut behind him and watched the truck disappear. Never would she see again the annoying but nice math professor whom she now wished she had never mocked or ignored.

"Oh my God!" exclaimed Josie. "He is not gay!" Anso, still in shock from having witnessed Brunrot's public removal, simply ignored what she considered merely one of Josie's various vocal speculations. So engulfed was she in the surreal insanity of the dark moment, she failed to notice how Josie had suddenly disappeared into the crowd before Anso could react.

"Josephine!" she called out, looking among the crowd, wondering what made her take off so abruptly.

After five minutes, she saw her up at the entrance of the school, talking with three of the large gray coats. One was smoking a cigarette, with his rifle slung across his back, as he looked at her with a hint of contempt.

Upon returning to the store, Anso found her father laboring in the back room on Major Engel's project. He had barely looked up as he seemed to not even notice his daughter's gaudy absence.

"I see you are working on the big frame!"

Her father simply looked up at her, saying nothing to her.

"Papa, you know they are not paying us, right? This is for the war effort!" She pronounced *war effort* mockingly, as she rolled her eyes. Anso's father stopped what he was doing and walked over toward her. He abruptly grabbed her chin, as though he was scolding a child.

"This is no time for your attitude! No time for your negativity! Your mouth can do more than hurt some feelings! Do not ever let me learn that you disrespected one of these soldiers who come into our store again!" He paused and stared at his daughter, unmoved by the shock in her eyes, before he continued his scolding.

"You just scurried out of here and just left that soldier here simply standing! Are you crazy! These are not elderly, day-to-day village people you are accustomed to disrespecting! These people are not to be played with or treated lightly, Anso!"

"God! First there is Monsieur Bourgeois and now you!? Is this entire city stacked with gutless cowards who just bend over and hand over their lives to these goddamn monsters!? Does nobody want to stand up to these scoundrels?" Anso demanded.

Once again, she regretted her sharp tongue and heart piercing words that seemed to escape her mouth before her mind could catch them. She knew her father had once faced the Germans before. He had faced them in Verdun, where he had lost his whole unit and was hit with mustard gas, and his physicality was affected to this day.

Gaston Chevalier appeared meek and quiet to many in the town. Born in 1890, he was older than most of the other fathers of Anso's friends, including Mayor Bourgeois. Like Anso, he was once energetic, loved the farm on which he raised just north in the Loire Valley, and loved playing with and corralling the animals on that farm. But just as he once tamed the animals on his farm, the great war of the new century had tamed him. That war, that was the first to see flying gunnery aircraft, rolling tanks, rapidly firing machine guns, had tamed not only Gaston Chevalier but in fact the entire country.

France had lost an entire generation in that war, and of all the nations plunged into the world's biggest, deadliest conflict in human history, France sustained the most casualties. Chevalier had lost his entire unit, gunned down between the diseased, cholera-filled trenches in what became known as no man's land. Gaston matured quickly and married just as rapidly. However, after his body had deteriorated from his exposure to German mustard gas, and he was clearly no longer the energetic man he once was, his wife immediately left him. Chevalier took up art and painting, a hobby that did not require too much movement to stress his already damaged nerves and senses.

He took up art as a craft and made a little money painting portraits for people. No longer able to manage the farm he inherited, he sold it and purchased a frame shop to help support himself as he painted. It was in this manner he would meet his second wife, and Anso's mother. The Fourniers were passing through town, on their way to Paris, when the family, impressed with Gaston's ability, thought it would be a good idea to have a portrait of their daughter painted. As smitten as Gaston was with the youngest daughter, he hesitated out of fear of her semi-abrasive and overprotective brother Charles. Charles was unlike most Frenchmen. Whereas most of the French did everything in moderation, he did things in slight excess, to include imbibing. Whereas most French could be disagreeable, Charles could be all-out abrasive and sometimes the use of fists was not uncommon.

Nonetheless, Charles oddly took to the polar opposite, now shy Gaston. Perhaps Charles could sense and appreciate that at one time Gaston shared Charles's passionate and combative spirit and that such a spirit that had been buried under the horror of that surreal war. Whatever it was, Gaston had a new life only a few years after the hideous events that had scarred and changed the course of his life.

However, he, and the rest of the country, never forgot the horrors of that war. Gaston, like most of the French, had no more appetite for war. A country once known historically for its military prowess under King Louis XIV, and a century and a half later under Napoleon Bonaparte, wanted nothing more to do with war.

Gaston listened to the stinging words of his daughter and understood her frustrations. It seemed like a lifetime ago, he would have felt the same. Though now, he, like many of the French of what remained of his broken generation, appreciated Germany's militaristic culture and the Germans' pride in their warlike history.

"Your mouth and complaining can get us killed! You have no idea what these people are capable of!" Monsieur Chevalier reiterated.

"Non! Papa! I have no idea! I just saw these monsters cart off Monsieur Brunrot! They are taking him for being homosexual!"

"You liked that professor, didn't you?" her father asked, his voice tender once again.

They embraced, and both looked out the window, wondering if the stories they heard about what happened in Poland were true.

Anso's father let her have the afternoon free, as he would be busy constructing the frame for Major Engel. She casually strolled down the street, as she once so oft liked to do. As desperately as she tried to enjoy what used to be her city, she could not help to notice the abundance of German soldier activity and red swastika flags hanging everywhere. When she came across her favorite boulangerie, she saw it closed down, boards on the windows, and

Mademoiselle Cohen was sitting on the sidewalk, her face buried in her hands, crying hysterically.

Anso slowly approached her, in an effort to comfort her.

"My husband and I built this store. It was given to us by my father." She sobbed.

"So, what happened?"

"The Germans have published an order that no Jewish person may run or operate a business. I have to close down!" Mademoiselle Cohen sobbed.

Anso tried to comfort her but had no bedside manner. Her embrace of Madamoiselle Cohen was awkward at best. Anso watched as Cohen slowly staggered away. She pitied her and could not help but notice how pathetic this proud lady once seemed. Anso wanted to believe that life would begin to ease its newfound constriction, but the constrictions only tightened. From the loss of her freedoms, to the imprisonment of Monsieur Brunrot, and now this.

She began to slump down against the wall of the now condemned boulangerie. Her once safe little world now seemed surreal and was beginning to overwhelm her. She felt herself struggling to draw in her breath. She felt beads of sweat bulleting on her forehead. Her heartbeat raced, and she was panicked. Her panic attack began to consume her, bury her, *helpessness*. She knew she was completely at the mercy of pure evil.

Suddenly her dog appeared from around the corner. The sight of Minou calmed her nerves, eased her breathing, and slowed her racing heartrate. She slowly held out her hand, lest she scare him off. As usual, he stopped and with long hesitation, studied the young woman trying to befriend him. Anso's mission to win the affection of Minou distracted her from her thoughts and preoccupations of the horror and misery surrounding her and swallowing her once untouchable little world.

Minou approached her cautiously and began to lick her fingers. She held her hand farther, joyous at the accomplishment at having finally won the little man's attention. Just as she held out her hand a little farther, it shook a little, startling Minou and sending him scampering off.

Anso decided to return to the shop to help her father. Later that afternoon, Anso and her father had completed the frame, and thus it was her father's turn to take an early break, leaving Anso to close the shop that evening. The German soldier, who had commissioned them with the task, came to procure it.

"This is very good workmanship for a French person," he quipped, unaware of the offense he just muttered.

"I think Major Engel will like it!"

"Wonderful, sir!" Anso muttered.

"Oh no! I am not a sir," the soldier politely corrected, confusing Anso.

"I am only Stabsgefreiter!" Still sensing confusion on Anso's face: "I am an administrative corporal and work directly as an admin clerk for the Major, and work as his driver."

"You mean, his errand boy." Once again, Anso's stinging words escaped without her even realizing it.

The corporal stared at her hard. Anso noticed that he did not share the same features as the other soldiers. He lacked the tall height, broad shoulders, and facial features. His face was round, and he himself was shorter and marginally portly.

He reached into his jacket and pulled out French currency.

"Here, for your work. It is all that I have!"

Anso gestured in a way with her hand, as if to indicate that he should not worry about it.

"No, really! I realize this is commissioned for the major, but I feel your father deserves something. Besides, I get paid next week. Here, take it! Please."

Anso slowly grabbed the money as she kept her eyes locked onto his. It was the first real interaction she had encountered with one of these soldiers. He was surprisingly human. Two German soldiers immediately interrupted the frozen moment, and the corporal regained his robotic posture as he sharply gestured toward the giant frame her father had just finished. Silently and quickly, the two Germans grabbed the frame and moved out the door and toward a large truck bearing the Nazi symbol, which seemed to take up the entire little narrow street.

Anso's stomach sank as she realized that could have been the same truck that had carted off Monsieur Brunrot to where, God only knew.

Suddenly, Mademoiselle Bourgeois burst through the door, not even realizing German soldiers were in there conducting business. The corporal slightly smiled in polite gesture and excused himself after he had seen his mission for Major Engel complete.

"Have you seen Josephine? She has been missing for hours!" Mademoiselle Bourgeois exclaimed.

"Not since they arrested Monsieur Brunrot. Then she cut through the crowd to go speak with the Germans!"

"She did what?" Mademoiselle gasped. "Why in the name of God would you let her do such a thing?"

"There I could do! Before I noticed she was even gone, I saw her up there talking with them! I figured she knew what she was doing, since you guys deal with these people on a daily basis!"

Mademoiselle Bourgeois stepped closer to Anso and coarsely replied,

"We do not *deal* with these people, young lady! They give us orders, and we obey. My husband crawls on his hands and knees for Engel in an effort to spare this city, and save those"—she began to sob—"to protect those with whom the Nazis disagree. But we cannot save everybody, you know. Monsieur Brunrot was simply too blatant to ignore. But for you ingrates to talk about us as if we are some kind of collaborators! How dare you!"

"Non! No, mademoiselle, I meant no such thing! I am sure everyone knows how much the mayor is trying to help. All I meant is that Josephine was probably more familiar in their dealings than those of us who have yet to barely step into their path. I am sure she will turn up. With all this going, she probably forgot she had duties at the office."

"Anso, you don't forget to honor your responsibilities to people like this! They thrive on strict obedience!"

"She will turn up!" Anso continued to insist.

Two days later, Josephine did show up.

Anso was working that morning in her shop, as usual. When she looked up from the counter, she saw Chantelle standing there.

"My God, I did not even hear you enter." Anso noticed a disturbed look on her face. "What is the matter!"

"Josephine is at the hospital! Her face is bruised, and she has been raped."

Anso quickly got up, abandoned all that she was doing, and made her way toward the door, even forgetting to lock it. When she arrived at the hospital, Josephine's families, along with Laurent, were already there. Laurent was desperately trying to hold her hand, but Josephine's hand would go limp as the effort to connect was not reciprocated. She would turn her bruised face and begin to quietly sob.

After so much time, she turned to Laurent.

"I am so sorry, sweetie! I never meant for this to happen!"

"It is not your—" Laurent tried to interject, but Josephine interrupted.

"No, listen! I tried to tell those soldiers that Monsieur Brunrot was not homosexual. I knew this because last year"—she paused, as though strategizing how to say this—"last year, we would sleep together."

Laurent's face went from sympathy to shock.

"It was before we were dating!" Josephine pathetically pleaded, but Laurent could only look away. His trophy girlfriend had secretly frolicked with the town homosexual, a man reputed not to be a man.

"I told those soldiers that they were mistaken. I told them how I knew..." Then she paused, heaving and trying to catch her breath to continue.

"They laughed. One of them grabbed me and told me"—another pause—"I needed to know what a real man felt like!" And she burst into tears and began shaking profusely.

Anso had never seen Josephine look this helpless and destroyed. Seeing her normally headstrong friend so hurt enraged Anso.

The mayor walked out, his head down. He could hear no more.

Anso could feel the rage well up inside her. Josephine was her friend, and these bullies had hurt her irreparably. She paced out after the mayor.

"Monsieur Bourgeois! We just cannot—" But the mayor interrupted her.

"We are not letting this happen," he said behind terse, gritted teeth. "I have been more than cooperative for the major, and he will make his soldiers account for this! This was not part of Petain's treaty!"

"I want to go with you!" Anso demanded.

The mayor paused. "Anso, given the combination of your temperament and how personally this touches us, I think that is a terrible idea"

"No, sir, I promise you, I will not say a word!" Anso pleaded.

The mayor paused and stared at her.

"Anso, you have a combative mouth. You cannot just say whatever comes to mind with these people. Their cruelty can be limitless."

They entered the huge lobby of the hotel de ville, their city hall. Anso recalled the many times as a little girl her father would walk her through the centuries-old building. She remembered thinking about the short, crudely dressed men who hoisted large, awkward, stone bricks back in the medieval times. She remembered wondering about how many trials took place throughout the past hundreds of years in this very hall. How many were condemned to be executed in the very foyer where Major Engel had addressed her city, sentencing them to his harsh rule under martial law. Anso remembered all the portraits of historical governmental figures that adorned the big halls. Now those portraits were gone and replaced with huge swastika flags. Anso looked at the other wall and was horrified. On the wall was a seven-foot framed picture of Adolf Hitler in a reverent pose that had him gazing up, as if heroically looking toward heaven. Anso's stomach instantly sank as she noticed the portrait was perfectly fitted in the frame her father had constructed.

They made their way up the stairs to the mayor's office, which was now occupied by Major Engel. The mayor knocked on the door that used to be his own. He timidly opened the door to see Major Engel sitting up straight at the desk, deeply engulfed in a book. He quickly looked up and upon seeing Monsieur Bourgeois, slowly arose from his chair and walked around to the front of the desk, where he perfectly postured himself, in his rigid stance, hands firmly behind his back. Anso noticed how much taller and imposing of a figure the major was to Mayor Bourgeois.

"Mr. Mayor, sir! As to what do I owe the honor of addressing you?" he asked in his crisp manner.

Monsieur Bourgeois was not so crisp. He was shaking, beads of sweat forming on his forehead.

"Sir, my daughter was raped." He declared, "And it was by your soldiers!"

The towering German officer kept his sterling posture, and even his composure, with the exception of a grimace and squinting of his eyes, as though he was attempting to understand what was being uttered to him.

The result of the meeting was that there was to be another mandatory meeting at 8 pm, where Monsieur Bourgeois would publicly confront those offenders who hurt his daughter.

The evening arrived swiftly, as the square was unusually packed, exactly like the first time the major addressed the helpless crowd. The soldiers, in their large coats and mirror-shined boots, stood with their weapons at the ready, peering out into the crowd from the bottom step. Captain Strobel was looking over them with his sadistic smile. Next to the door of the church, Major Engel was speaking with a young lieutenant with a boyish face. Not far from where he was talking was a table with the three German soldiers who had raped Josephine. They were not wearing their gray coats but were wearing their dress uniforms. They all looked nervous. Finally, the major walked onto the patio and addressed the crowd after what seemed an eternity.

"Ladies and gentlemen! Once again, I plead for your forgiveness in my interruption of your conveniences!"

There was that word again, *conveniences*! After compelling every person out of their homes for the second time to bear witness to a rape trial, it was merely a disturbance of conveniences.

"We, unfortunately, have a grave situation at hand that must be dealt with immediately. An accusation has been brought to my attention. An accusation dealing with some soldiers in my sturm." With that, the major slightly motioned for the mayor to come up the stairs and join him and Captain Strobel.

Bourgeois slowly made his way up the stairs, followed by Laurent and Josephine's brother, as the guarding soldiers slightly moved to allow him just enough space, never removing their gaze from the crowd.

Engel greeted Bourgeois with only a stern look.

"Sir, are these the soldiers you claim violated your daughter?"

Bourgeois looked nervously down at Josephine and turned to look at Major Engel and cautiously bit his lip and nodded his head.

"And, sir, you wish to bring accusation here publicly? Is this correct?"

Bourgeois paused. Anso looked on horrified at the mayor's hesitance. She shook her head, in some vain hope that by nodding her head, some connection would shake his head as well.

Finally, but slowly, Bourgeois conceded.

"Very well." And the Major walked to the edge looking out over the crowd. He slowly and deliberately extracted his sidearm, which was equally as shined and well-kept as the boots he was wearing. He turned toward Bourgeois, slowly raising his sidearm.

Anso saw the centuries-old wall of the church sprayed with his blood, fragments of his skull, and pieces of his brain before the blast rang out over the gasping crowd.

The rest took place in slow motion. Josephine's brother rushed to catch his collapsing father. He did not so much as see a grinning Captain Strobel turn to aim his pistol right at his forehead. By the time the crowd heard the thump of her brother hit the ground, accompanied by Josephine's screams, Strobel was smiling as he pointed his weapon point blank at Laurent.

Josephine and her mother were blocked by the soldiers guarding the steps as they feebly attempted to charge the stage. Without so much as breaking his stance, the major holstered his pistol and nodded at one of the guards to allow the family access.

While Mademoiselle Bourgeois was caressing the raptured head of her husband, the former mayor, Engel addressed the crowd.

"Now, does anyone else choose to lob accusation against the soldiers within my sturm?" he sternly asked, as though he were merely a teacher scolding his class.

"I have attempted valiantly to exercise patience with you! I have attempted to conduct my operations with minimal disruptions to your daily functions! Yet you test me with your arrogant lawlessness. Let me be clear! You can choose to cooperate and make this process easy, or you can choose to make this as painful as possible! But only know that I will not waver in my mission, and our cause will be supported." He quickly spun around, his hands still planted behind his back.

He stopped, turned back toward the crowd. "Tonight's curfew will begin effective immediately! With exception of the family mourning." He moved his eyes toward a sobbing, broken Josephine and her mother.

"They are permitted to be out to make arrangements indefinite throughout the evening."

Major Engel had not only shattered Bourgeois's skull with that blast but Anso's belief in humanity. The round in his sidearm wiped clean a man's life, and Anso's faith in humanity with it. No longer would she ever believe that the depth of human depravity was hinging upon the derangement of the society. Tonight she understood that humanity was rotten on all levels.

After all, the Germans were one of the most advanced societies of the time and had led civilization throughout the past half of the millennium. Almost every great classical composer came out of Germany, Mozart, Brahms, Schumann, Bach, and Beethoven. Every great scientist who defined the advancement of physics came out of Germany. Germany produced Johan Kepler, the scientist who discovered the planetary motions in the 1500s, and even that time, produced great scientists such as Werner Heisenberg, presently a young, forty-year-old physicist, a pioneer in quantum physics.

Even Major Engel was impressive. His manners were humble, his movements crisp, and his articulation sophisticated. Even as he blew out a man's brains in front of his family, he conducted himself with the utmost class. The Germans themselves conducted themselves with discipline, whether in their duties or out in sipping beer in the restaurants. Their professional demeanor and sophisticated leadership eradicated any stereotypical, typical view of carousing, boisterous, drunken soldiers. Never were any of the Germans in Engel's sturm seen even glassy eyed. Anything more than moderate consumption would have invited scrutiny from Major Engel and sadistic wrath from the masochistic Strobel, his second in command.

Yet for all their grace, class, wonderful history, and spearheading of civilization, Germany had become the face of evil. Their army, and the leaders who governed over it, would be etched and branded in the future as the personification of human evil. It would serve as solid evidence that humanity at its root was evil to the core, no matter how civilized they aspired to be. The worst animals could never mimic the bestial cruelty of the Nazi empire.

Days later, Josephine had committed suicide. The guilt she shouldered for her belief that she was the cause of her brother's and father's deaths was too much for her to take. In a short span of a week, Mademoiselle Bourgeois had lost her entire family.

Months passed and then a year. The citizens went timidly about their day-to-day routine. Engel had made his point, and made it forcefully. The Germans were not to be disobeyed. The Germans were not to be even discreetly or indirectly opposed. Over the next year, dozens were arrested for suspicions of being Jewish or harboring Communist sympathies. Jealous husbands could report their wives' lovers to Captain Strobel, and that afternoon, they were arrested while eating in a restaurant. The Germans always arrested people in public. If a report came at night before curfew, then the Wehrmacht waited until the next morning. Public arrests disarmed the accused and further imposed the idea that the Wehrmacht would not be opposed, or even slowed down. It further branded the fear within the citizenry and reinforced the idea that dissidents would be found and would be arrested. It was never rare for German soldiers to inspect those being arrested on suspicion of being Jewish. The accused stood up and removed his pants and undergarments in the gawking presence of the onlookers, consisting of women and children, for the German to inspect for the undeniable evidence of Judaism. Those with penises still intact were still taken away, even after exposing themselves to the town and proving they were not cut. The Wehrmacht offered no such luxury as due process or trials. They had no time for such inconveniences.

One simple day at school could be a fateful, life-altering day, on the cruel whim of Captain Strobel. This was what happened on a day Mademoiselle Depres was teaching math class, in the eerie absence of the former beloved, if not gossiped about, Monsieur Brunrot.

Mademoiselle Depres tried to conduct classes as usual, but the mood was anything but usual. An eerie cloud had permeated over the now frightened class. No longer did there exists any playfully exchanged glances. The normally disobedient French adolescents were now stone-cold silent and stared straight ahead, not really absorbing the lesson but dreading what would happen once they stepped back out into Germany's lair, what used to be their own streets. Bone-chilling fear had now replaced the secret mischief that had always lingered over the strict air of French classrooms.

If Depres's hesitant style of teaching was not awkward enough, a jolting harsh knock on the door interrupted an already flustered Depres, and a German lieutenant entered the room, followed by three soldiers in their gray coats and their black helmets. Depres was already frightened into shock, as a visit from these men on Strobel's directive was never good news. However, the youthful baby face of the oberleutnant, otherwise known as a first lieutenant, froze her in her tracks. Young Benzinger looked almost as though he could be one of her students, still with acne scars and cheeks composed of baby fat. The young lieutenant pulled the teacher aside and spoke quietly to her. She could not get over how young he looked. But for the severity of the situation, she may have otherwise laughed at this young, adolescent-looking soldier in an oversized coat, with weapon slung over his back.

Mademoiselle Depres obediently stepped aside and allowed a young boy, who appeared no older than the rest of the pupils who were helpless under the gaze of the imposing black helmets, under whose brim their hidden eyes scornfully gazed.

"Class!" the young soldier commanded. "I am Lieutenant Benzinger! I will need all the boys to line up against the chalkboard! My soldiers will direct you from there!" With that, Lieutenant Benzinger stepped back as a soldier helped hurry the scared kids against the board. The soldier then motioned with his hand, and the boys slowly, and with hesitation, dropped their pants, exposing their penis in front of the teacher who was looking away, attempting not to sob, and the girls, who were looking down, in attempt not to take advantage of the awful circumstance. Their discipline succeeded, until a man's sob broke out, ringing through the frightful silence of the classroom. Jean Luc began to cry uncontrollably. The girls looked up and saw the German's burrowed brow and his eyes light up in a disgusted frown.

Now all the discipline in the world now could not keep the girls and the teacher from looking down to see what had sparked the fearsome Germans' unrelenting interests. They looked to see a circumcised penis hanging from the massive body of what was once a much feared and antagonistic but frightened and now humiliated Jean Luc. The pupils' stomachs instantly dropped as they all simultaneously felt hopeless out of a helpless pity for the poor kid who once was the imposing man who terrorized them only months prior. A Jewish kid could hide his religion, but a circumcised penis did not lie. Jean Luc was a jew.

Only a situation so dreadful and occupiers so perverse as Engel's Wehrmacht could in the span of a millisecond render a young hoodlum like Jean Luc someone to pity and for whom they now had concerned endless compassion. With a snap of his fingers, and a quick nod of his head, the German soldier motioned for the kids to pull their pants back up, and two of the gray coats forcefully grabbed a slumping Jean Luc by each arm and escorted a sobbing Jean Luc out of the room and out of their lives forever. Benzinger then stepped up to the teacher.

"Mademoiselle, I am afraid I must escort you to the headmaster's office, where the two of you will need to speak with Captain Strobel and answer charges of harboring Jews in your school." Benzinger spoke with an almost childlike compassion.

The class could see the teacher's legs shake, as was understandable at the mention of any encounter with Captain Strobel, especially a charge of this gravity. The young lieutenant led the frightened teacher down the hallway. They passed the library where another one of Benzinger's soldiers were going through the card catalog to inspect for any authors or literary works now banned by the Wehrmacht. Benzinger's soldiers were now overseeing the class. The teacher could not even discipline the class and could do nothing to save one of her students, as reviled as he was, from fatal harm. Helplessness.

As a year passed, these extreme incidences began to subside. The Germans were content that most of those who were Jewish, homosexual, or Communists had been apprehended and sent away. However, one evening after curfew, Anso heard commotion a few doors down, where Genevieve and the Benoit family had been staying with Chantelle's family. She could hear the voice of Mademoiselle Benoit and the overriding harsh commands of men's voices in the coarse-sounding German language.

"Please!" she could hear Mademoiselle Benoit continue to beg. Anso rushed outside and was immediately met by a German soldier who put up his hand and ordered her back inside. Ignoring the order, she looked over and saw Lieutenant Benzinger holding up his hands, politely trying to calm her. Imposing red flashing lights from the truck illuminated the otherwise blacked-out street, making everyone's faces visible. Out of the apartment door, a German soldier escorted little Adrienne. Adrienne tried her best to keep her German escort's rapid pace as she dragged one foot, and one hand was limp and motionless. Adrienne was the only one who did not have a bewildered look of frozen fear but instead, a bewildered look of confusion.

The Germans had begun to comb through medical records and take into custody the handicapped to euthanize them in their effort to rebuild the perfect society. As the German soldier continued to drag poor Adrienne toward the truck, two soldiers opened up the back gate to make way for her.

"Maman, nous allons ou? Nous allons ou, maman?" cried a confused and now frightened Adrienne. Tonight would be the first time in a decade and a half when Adrienne was not guided and physically escorted by her doting mother. All of Adrienne's young life, she was taken to every appointment in town by her mother, constantly under her careful watchful eye. For tonight, all the doting mother could do was bury her face in her husband's shoulder and cry, as a young, naivelLieutenant Benzinger tried his best to minimize and comfort her.

Anso heard the clank of the metal doors and one last pathetic plea from Adrienne, now obviously frightened, "Maman, nous allons ou?" And then the red brake lights ceased, and the darkness returned as the truck sped off. Only Adrienne's frightened pleas filled the black night, replaced by Mademoiselle Benoit's muffled crying into her husband's shoulder. Helplessness.

Two

REGRET

R egret is one of the most powerful and overwhelming presences a human soul can shoulder. It is the burden of that which one can never change, the past. One may always change their current situation, and may always alter their future, but the past is always there. Unchanged, unaltered, and always humbling.

I sit in front of a row of forty-four people from all walks of life. Fulton County is a strange jurisdiction, as it is shaped like an hourglass, an hourglass piercing through the circle of Interstate 285, the perimeter that encloses upon this ever-expanding city. Each time we try people from the inner city of Atlanta, their juries consist of nothing but the most affluent suburban residents of Roswell and Alpharetta, as very few in the inner-city bother to show for jury duty, if they even get the summons. Such contorted county geography, as a result of decades-old gerrymandering, has made my job one of the easiest. It takes little effort to convince twelve jurors from the safe, sheltered subdivisions of upper 400, to convict the dangerous animal from the streets who sits in before them. For their only exposure to black inner-city youth are those they see on television recruited to their favorite college football teams. To these jurors, "that Jontorious, what's his name" is the kid with the earring who ran the winning touchdown for UGA. Outside of that, however, the defendant, usually a massive black youth, who stares straight ahead with an emotionless scowl, is simply one of those thugs who haunts the pretty streets of downtown with his pants hanging down below his ass, probably aspiring to be in a gang or, if not, aspiring to be a rapper, screaming belligerent profanities, glorifying such. My job is practically done, and little effort is required to convict.

The rooms of the superior court of Fulton County are well-kept. Polished fine wood that makes up the bench, recorder's desk, and witness stand encompassed by soft carpeted walls, adorned with framed portraits of former judges, many of whom went on to serve on the Georgia Supreme Court or on one of the Federal benches. Within these walls is a neatly concealed door, behind where the bailiff sits, during the proceedings.

Behind this door, the conditions are exactly the opposite. Behind this door is the stank, urine-stench holding cell, where jump-suited inmates sit for hours that can seem eternal, with nothing to do but stare at the walls or the sheriff's deputies tasked with guarding them.

The bailiff, a sheriff's deputy, sits comfortably in his chair, at the side of the room. As the door opens, he struggles to jump up as his peer, another court sheriff, escorts a gangly, awkward Michael Parent toward the defense team's table. Parent looks almost ridiculous in an oversized suit his mother bought him and that the county allows defendants to wear for trial. Young Michael stares shamefully down at the floor. I wonder if he realizes how open and shut of a case this is. I wonder if he realizes that his young, small life is about to take a drastic, disastrous turn for the ultimate worse. I feel as though I am watching a horrific auto wreck occur in which none of the parties realize they will be dragged from the jaws of life, permanently paralyzed. I wonder if he thinks about how his life will never be the same. He will spend the formative years of his young adulthood in a jumpsuit, probably being someone's girlfriend, until he fully develops physically. His mental and emotional development will be forever capped, and this will be the next fifteen years of his life. Upon release, he will be forced to live under a bridge, as no renter will be allowed to rent him even a one-room space in the ghetto. Every living accommodation will be off limits to him, as they will fall within three miles of a school or park. He will be a modern-day leper.

This is only conditional upon if he survives his long fifteen to twenty years in a state prison. Convicts incarcerated for sex crimes are absolutely at the bottom of the food chain, dominated by killers, gang members, and white collar criminals, whom most criminals regard as smart and able to circumvent a system no better than their own depraved locked-down society.

I look back at the helpless mother and father. The father has a stern grimace, and he is likewise staring down at the floor, attempting in vain not to cry. They realize they are not at a trial but an execution, a slow, deliberate, tortuous execution.

"All rise!" commands a feeble voice, attempting to sound authoritative. The extremely portly sheriff who a minute prior was comfortably nestled and tucked behind the desk is now standing in front of the bench, facing the people, as his command completely jars me from my thoughts.

"The Honorable Harry Beckford presiding!" The sheriff momentarily stands at attention, then resumes his place behind his desk as a thin, older man casually waves his hand and tells the crowd, "Please take your seats, ladies and gentlemen! Sit down!" in a laid-back, Southern gentlemanly voice. He takes his seat at the bench and puts on heavy-rimmed glasses that seem to overtake his tiny bald head. The court attendant hands him a paper, and he studies the docket out of the corner of those glasses.

"Okay, so we have the case of State versus Parent." He continues to study the docket. "Yes, that is correct, a stat rape case. Okay. Mr. McCullough, how are you today?"

"Good, sir," my colleague stands up to declare, quickly taking his seat.

He glances my way.

"Mr. Carlson, and how are you today, sir?"

I quickly interrupt him before he can finish as I abruptly stand.

"Your Honor! I apologize!" I shout, not even realizing it. Judge Beckford does not break his stern glance he maintains in my direction out of the corner of his glasses.

"Your Honor, with all apologies"—my legs now feel as though they are about to give out from under me—"At this time, the state would like to drop all pending charges against defendant, Michael Rutherford Parent." I swallow hard and force what little bile my mouth can produce to pass down, to wet my now burning-dry throat.

The judge breaks his gaze that held me captive and stares out front of him as his jaw slowly drops. A look of confusion overtakes him.

"Okay!" He looks around, confused. Judges hate to be surprised; judges hate to feel as though they have been ambushed. He clears his throat.

"Well, then, I suppose this case is dismissed!" He smiles nervously, as though he were just caught with his pants down.

"Well, the good news is that we have one case less on the docket!" He then recasts his glare toward me.

"I would like to see you in my chambers for a minute, sir!" And with that, he taps the gavel. I know that I am in trouble. I can feel the presence of my boss in my peripheral vision. I can feel his angry, penetrating stare from in the seats behind me. My boss is the Fulton County district attorney, or what we call the DA. Regret!

Weeks before, I had tried to beg him to drop these charges. "No, we need to proceed with the case!" he said as casually as if he were ordering coffee. Never was there a case that DA Raul Brown did not want to vehemently prosecute.

"Sir, if you are worried about keeping me busy, I would not be concerned about a lack of crimes to try in southwest Atlanta," I said jokingly. "You know, crimes that involve victims, and maybe a firearm to boot!" Paul glared at me unamused. Both the Dekalb and Fulton County district attorneys were always in a competition to see which one could bury enough kids under their system. Both of their counties had a big piece of the poorer sides of western and southside of Atlanta. Both of their counties had high crime, and each knew that a wave of punishment leading to diminishment thereof could be a launching pad for their political and legal careers. Little did they realize that incarcerating youth only triples crime. Our criminal justice system was a drug in its own right; one taste and a young person was forever immersed it its survival-oriented culture. Their contacts on the street quadrupled, as many were compelled to join a gang to survive, and their allegiance never ended when they left those barbwire gates.

Dekalb County was infamous for its harsh sentencing of young offenders. What always stunned me was that whether it the Dekalb or Fulton County DAs or the Georgia attorney general, all of who were black, they were always the toughest and most cruel on those with whom one would think they would sympathize. Their stories could almost be identical. They grew up in run-down neighborhoods around Bankhead or College Park and attended Morehouse University, and many of them received scholarships or grants to go to the DC area to attend Howard Law School. They came back to Atlanta and joined the state district attorney's office of their respective counties. Even in the rare cases, where Georgia state law gave prosecutors and judges' leeway, their sentencing recommendations were the most unbending and harsh. I always wondered about that. Those I always thought would be more sympathetic to these kids' backgrounds whose story they once shared were usually the most unforgiving. In an age where we constantly hear about white privilege, who could never understand the plight of these poor perpetrators, it was their fellow brethren that burned them the worst in the courtroom.

I know at some point in the course of the afternoon, I am going to have to face Paul. I swipe my card and enter the old building on Marietta Street next to the Phillips Arena.

"Hey!" the older Jamaican lights up behind the desk as I greet her each morning.

"How are the kids?"

"Oh! They are so well, thank you!" Her voice rises in joy at the thought of them. Then her voice gets serious. "Oh! Shannon! By the way, Mr. Paul is looking for you!"

"OK! I will go talk to him," I say, trying to sound casual. Trying to mask my utter terror at what penalty awaits me for my public disregard of his order.

The next day, I wait until after five to go up and clean out my desk, so as to avoid the uncomfortable attention my firing would generate. More than losing my job, I dread the sympathy, or the *what were you thinking?* looks, as the know-it-alls shake their heads, holding coffee cups that seem to never leave their hands. I figure it is no big deal; I will find another job soon enough. Even if I have to bartend in the meantime. Days pass by, and I do not worry too much about it. After weeks pass, I begin to panic. My savings from my time in Afghanistan begins to dwindle. Then it is gone. More weeks begin to pass. Before college, it was easy to apply to restaurants. I just walked in and filled out an application and was working that afternoon. More than a decade later, I am lucky if I could even find a "Now hiring" sign. On the few occasions that I could, I would see either dozens of kids filling out applications, or the manager would take it and want me to come back for a second interview. A second interview? This is barely a minimum-wage job, whose compensation was in tips, dependent upon the kindness of strangers, and today these jobs are treated as though they are $50,000 careers with full benefits packages.

As time progresses, my indefinite, eternal unemployment seems permanent, which defines life of post-2010. As my motivation to earn money decreases, my alcohol intake increases. I begin to sleep in. Facebook becomes my only outlet to the world, and my only means of socializing. Social media provides my only lifeline to the outside world, without having to actually be in it.

My days pass, and I watch people progress, their lives continue, as I have nothing to do but sit in my room and drink. Absentia opportunities, chance, or a life, my own freedom is slipping away from me. The bottle becomes my sole escape from the prison in which I have found myself. While initially I thought my penalty or disobeying Mr. Paul was termination, I begin to realize that in this country today, in this economy, termination has grown to akin to incarceration. I begin to rue the day that I stood up for young Michael. To hell with him, I should have let him rot. It is not my problem if he had to suck some fat man's dick for the rest of his young life, but I made it my problem. *Regret*.

My wife has become the sole bread winner. We quit sleeping together, and I try to avoid her at all cost. I try to avoid myself at all costs. I awake groggily around ten as usual. I try a few calisthenics to get the blood pumping and shamefully toss the empty bottles that I cannot believe I was able to consume the night before. As usual, the first order of business is to pound some water, then OJ, and then sip my first of what would be many steaming cups of coffee.

As I slowly make my way to the kitchen, my wife is in the kitchen, perky and watching television. Shit! It is her day off. I forgot. As usual, I try to make my way around our condo as silently as possible. She shoots a glare my way, and her face instantly turns from perky to sour. Still groggy, and yet to have made my trip to the bathroom to relieve last night's indulgence, I have to first endure, once again, my wife's shaming.

I try to ignore her but feel the wrath and disgust of her gaze, making my headache that much more intense.

"You realize you are in trouble, right?

I look at her, confused.

"Making racist comments on Facebook? Shannon, are you out of your mind?"

I can see her register the stunned look on my face.

"Oh, you were so lit, you probably don't remember?" And she turns around, sighing in disgust.

Most nights I do spend online, my only portal to what was once a life. Usually around midnight, my memory gets hazy. I could never tell you what I wrote after one am. Apparently, I got into a troll fest online, and who knows what I said.

Regret is when we allow the world to hear what is really on our minds. I think of Mademoiselle Benoit. I know her regret had to be heavier than mine was for my online racist comment.

Loire Valley, France, late 1941

Anso knew that it was only a matter of time before the Wehrmacht came for little Thomas. In the days since they took little Adrienne into custody, Mademoiselle Benoit had grown despondent. She was rarely seen out in the streets. Meanwhile, German presence had become so commonplace in the streets of her city she rarely noticed their day-to-day activities. From time to time, she would shudder to think that seeing soldiers with bright swastika armbands, as she had for the past year and a half, had now become all too normal. However, it was the deprivation to which she never grew accustomed. She missed being able to casually waltz into whatever restaurant she wished. Now, some were strictly off limits, and available only to Germans.

During this time, while Anso was growing disturbingly accustomed to German presence, Mademoiselle Benoit was becoming more erratic. She would be caught out in the streets, dressed poorly and oft times talking to herself. Genevieve reported a much more horrific story. At home, Mademoiselle Benoit would be curled up in the fetal position, sometimes screaming.

Then late one evening, it happened. Everybody saw it coming, but it, nonetheless, shocked everyone on Anso's street. It was well after the German-mandated curfew, and the small city had gone black. Small reading lamps lit the rooms of those French unable to sleep and radiated a silent room that was once filled by radio programming, before the Germans ordered all radios confiscated. That evening the silence was broken by a shrill scream coming from the Etiennes' apartment a few doors down from Anso. The screams continued and seemed to be growing louder and more bloodcurling. Concern churning in her gut, Anso darted out of the apartment in the pitch-black darkness, pumping adrenaline burying all such fear that she may encounter a Wehrmacht soldier and be killed.

She sprinted the few doors down and noticed that she was ducking her head, realizing how absurd that was, when she stopped to knock.

Before she could even finish knocking, the door wildly swung open, and Anso could not so much as see who was opening it nor who had grabbed her shirt and dragged her inside. Mademoiselle Benoit was crouched in a corner shaking in the fetal position. Anso had known that Adrienne's arrest and transport to execution weighed heavily on her. How could it not? Yet to see it unfolding in Benoit's psychotic state took the breath out of Anso. Never had she seen a grown woman literally lose her mind. Benoit began shaking profusely. Her shaking turned to convulsions. She began uttering in gibberish, as though she were attempting to speak in multiple tongues. Genevieve tried frantically to calm her down, and her repeated shushes and whispering seemed to simmer her mother's frantic state somewhat.

Tears rolled down her once beautiful face before the stress of occupation had wrinkled and sunk her cheeks. She began to breathe heavily but slowly.

"It is all my fault" she confessed in a voice hoarse from her screaming.

"What are you talking about, Maman?" Genevieve innocently inquired.

"Your sister! I did this to her! I gave her away!" her mother sobbed.

"No, maman! You were a great mother! You took care of your children, we loved you. I still love you. And Adrienne loved you so much! You did not do anything! The Germans made you give her up! There was nothing you could do!" Genevieve attempted in vain to assure her.

"No! You don't understand!" Mademoiselle protested as she looked away in tears, "I wished for this day! I so many times wished for this day, and God punished me by granting this day!"

"Maman, I don't understand!" Genevieve said, looking surprised.

"I used to sometimes wish she would die. I was so selfish, but caring for her 24/7 became exhausting. I used to have to help her to the bathroom and dreaded the life she would struggle to live, a life without a man in her life, a life of helplessness. But I wished this also because I was selfish. I dreaded a life of having to take complete care of someone so helpless..."

"No, Mother! You did a good job with her!" Genevieve interrupted.

"Mademoiselle, we all get frustrated. Sometimes, I get frustrated with Thomas, " Anso tried to reason. She could imagine Mademoiselle at times selfishly wishing that Adrienne was gone, and she would be free from worry, the work, and the helplessness. Now her wish had returned to haunt her. Regret.

Then she stopped and wondered. Did her father, Monsieur Chevalier, ever wish Thomas would just die? It seemed selfish. On the other hand, when witnessing the day-to-day struggle some had to endure, was wishing they were dead cruel or humane? Were there times when the lines between cruelty and humanity crossed and became one? Did the Germans feel as though they were doing the right thing? Regret.

"You cannot know what was in my head!" Mademoiselle protested to Anso and Genevieve. "This is all my fault!" She resumed her frantic screaming.

As Genevieve hugged her to try to calm her, her mother began to laugh nervously and in a frantic chatter. Her eyes lit up in an expression neither Anso nor Genevieve had ever witnessed from Mademoiselle Benoit, as though she were possessed. Genevieve continued to hug her and resumed trying to calm her hysterical mother, only to have her mother throw her off in such a violent fit that Genevieve was hurled across the room and knocked over a tabl, as she hit the wall. Anso tried to rush forward but stopped in her tracks when Mademoiselle Benoit shot up.

"Je suis desolee, ma cherie!" she kept chanting. "I am so sorry, my darling! I will be punished for wishing this on you, my baby!" And with that, she bolted to the door, swung it frantically open, and charged out in the darkness, screaming like a banshee.

Genevieve got up from her knelt position, throwing Anso off of her, as Anso tried to stop her.

"You can't go out there!" Anso tried to remind her best friend, only to be thrown off once more.

During their grappling match, harsh German commands could be heard beyond the open door that answered Mademoiselle's erratic screaming. When their commands went unanswered, her screams were met by the sound of crisp, rapid gunfire. Then her screams went silent.

Genevieve rushed toward the door. Anso chased after her and again grabbed her shoulders, but in vain, as Genevieve was able to throw her off, leaving Anso helpless in the threshold of the doorway. Anso watched as her best friend became but a shadowy silhouetted figure becoming ever so distant. Anso again heard the barking of commands in that harsh, consonant-laden German language. From the doorstep, Anso then saw the flash of a muzzle, followed by the sound of a firing burst, and the shadowy figure paused, as though frozen in time, and then dropped. Anso's best friend had been shot dead as she watched, paralyzed and stranded from the door. Regret.

Three

RAGE

Rage. The anger that burns so deeply within you—you feel it replace your blood, coursing through your veins, accelerating your heartbeat, flowing up to your mind, and clouding your judgment in immediate impulse.

My appointment with the head of the Georgia bar ethics committee is this morning. My former boss reported me to the state bar for "making racist public comments." One evening, after too many drinks, I got on Facebook. I commented on some posts, which led to an accusation toward my old boss that if young Mike Parent was black, he would not have insisted to viciously prosecute him. Another post was an argument over Obama's economy. Not being able to find work gave the time to drink and obsess. I would comment on anything that made me angry, which could very well be anything.

The head of the ethics committee was the former chief justice of the supreme court of the state of Georgia. He was a small but bulky black man, around the age of sixty. His claim to fame was that as a young, freshly graduated attorney, he clerked for Justice Thurgood Marshall, one of the first black justices on the Supreme Court and the attorney who argued *Brown v Board of Education* in front of the US Supreme Court in 1954.

I sit in front of the desk as I look at a printed copy of my post. I had responded to someone's post praising the president. I sit and painfully go through the back-and-forth, my scathing comments and the various black commenters who defended him to the core.

Finally, I read my last comments on the thread. Those forgotten, blacked-out words, with my picture next to it.

"This has been the worst economy we have seen"

The next comment is by a guy named Marcus.

"Try unemployment down to 7% you fool"

I then look at my picture of me in a suit, smiling in front of the Georgia capitol. The quote next to it pathetically states, "Well I haven't worked for over eight months"

The following comment is placed next to a picture of a black guy standing in front of his car. His name is LeRoy. "LOL! See, you white guys aren't runnin' the show anymore! Obama done come and put you in your place, and now your clown ass is all mad an' shit, and yous wanna blame Obama!"

My last comment is the most difficult to read.

I try to gulp, but my dehydrated throat is dry from this morning's quick screwdriver, and all I can feel is the sandpaper taste of a parched throat. I look down at the comment that reads:

"yeah! I know! LOL! typical black guy response. Maybe that attitude is why you people (and you know what I mean by "you people") own the incarceration rate, own the poverty rate, and own the unemployment rate! Oh, but that's right! Its white privilege! What a frickin joke! You have a black president, black attorney general, blacks serve in the senate, congress, have served as the highest ranking billet of the uniformed armed services, Chairman of the Joints Chiefs of Staff, I could go on. And who do Indian people, Asians, Arabs, have representing them? Right! Nobody! And yet, they are running like and engine! And if you ever call me a clown again, ..."

I put down the page before I could read the N-word I had posted on the world wide web. The pause I take seems like an eternity, but I finally muster up the courage to look at Chief Justice Steven Grey, who sits across the desk with a fiery look in his eye. My eye meets his, and I hold his look just long enough so that I can immediately look away. My self-worth melts away with each second of gazing into his disgusted, angry eyes. After too long a moment of awkward silence, the chief justice clears his throat and begins to speak in a voice that reminds me of James Earl Jones's.

"I must say, you have disappointed us all, Mr. Carlson. We all had such high hopes for you. We all were looking forward to the career you would polish! We waited in anxious hope that you would step into the big shoes of your grandfather."

Et voila! There it is. Finally, the lecture I have awaited for days, the great comparison to my mighty grandfather.

My grandfather was more than just a circuit judge. To avoid the Great Depression, Victor Carlson joined the FBI. After pursuing so many cold cases of citizens fleeing the draft, he decided to enlist himself in the infantry as a paratrooper. Upon his return, he used the Montgomery GI bill to attend law school and went on to a promising career as a local prosecutor, in the steps of his father.

However, something struck him in his short years prosecuting criminals. During the early 1950s, he began to witness something that he had failed to notice during the Depression, or as a kid. He grew appalled at the hideous, animal-like treatment black people received. He would squirm whenever he witnessed a brave black soul who tried to enter a restaurant, only to hear, "Sorry sir, we don't serve negroes in here!" Cruelty so polite, as it always appeared to be, as a young Anso learned when her city was run by Major Engel, or when I had to inform young Mike's family that his fate was sealed.

Victor began eating in restaurants set aside only for blacks, riding the back of the bus with them. He eventually quit his job as the prosecutor and became a prominent civil rights attorney. He could not fathom how a country could send so many kids to their deaths fighting something as grotesque as Nazism, only to permit something as equally hideous as Jim Crow here in their own country.

The irony of my grandfather's new war was that he descended from a family that epitomized the Southern, wealthy, white landowner family. The family came to the US in the 1600s.

In 1593, William Carlson, then a young Briton, had spent an uneventful youth as a horse trader. By the time he had taken up with Raleigh, he had long been warned about his association with the troublemaking Walter Raleigh. Yet William understood the financial and political opportunity that came with being one of Raleigh's associates, as Raleigh himself was secretly sexually engaged with Queen Elizabeth the first, one of Britain's most powerful monarchs, and also referred to as the Virgin Queen for her refusal to choose a royal spouse. Raleigh was trouble, though, and when he married one of Elizabeth's lady servants, that enraged the queen, and such a scandal sent tremors throughout the country. Nevertheless, upon release from his imprisonment at the tower, the queen granted Raleigh patent on the recently colonized new land, as well as a royal charter, and Raleigh and Carlson got to escape the very social storm that he himself had caused. Raleigh sent Carlson to the North American colony that had now been named Virginia, while Raleigh himself coasted to South America. Raleigh returned to England, having informed the maddened queen that the colony was named Virginia, after the Virgin Queen, even though the natives had called that land Wingina, after a tribal, and now regional, ruler.

Meanwhile, Carlson had stayed behind for a while in the Virginia colony, never to rejoin Raleigh until after the Queen's death in 1603. His companion, Raleigh, had returned to England to help stage a revolt against Elizabeth's succeeding monarch, King James I. Raleigh was immediately imprisoned in the tower once more and was released on the condition that he find for the king the streets of gold that Raleigh himself had embellished to the previous queen, concerning his travels to South America. The grossly exaggerated writing had led to the book *El Dorado*, whose legend became an obsession to most European royalty, and now Raleigh was committed to find the fabled and fictional treasure. Not wanting to admit the falsity of his correspondence, and certainly not wanting to disappoint the king, whose trust he desperately needed to earn, Raleigh sought out the only friend he ever truly trusted, Carlson. After months of frustrated search for golden streets that did not exist, Raleigh stormed a Spanish fortress in South America, with Carlson loyally accompanying him.

After the successful raid, producing enough gold for Raleigh to take back and satisfy the king, thus returning Raleigh to the king's good graces, Raleigh returned to England. Carlson, however, opted to return to the land he had begun to cultivate, his newfound home in the colony of Virginia. Good for Carlson that he decided such, as Raleigh was apprehended immediately upon his return to England. After receiving dispatch of the siege of one of his fortresses in South America, King Phillip III of Spain grew enraged, nearly erratic. That anyone would dare commit such a brazen act, thus challenging his reign of authority in his colony, when he had been so careful about maneuvering north for fear of encroaching upon King Charles's colony in the mid-Atlantic part of North America. Seeking satisfaction, King Phillip angrily demanded that King Charles take care of Raleigh at once. Charles, not wanting to anger Spain, nor the mighty Austrian Hapsburg Empire, from whom Phillip was born, as well as seeking a good reason to rid himself of this troublesome adventurer, gladly acquiesced.

Lucky for Carlson that he had detoured to North America, for as Raleigh's companion, he was wanted by the king also. Fortunately, he was not wanted quite enough to warrant dispatching soldiers in the dreaded wilderness that was the king's colonies, and Carlson knew better than to ever return to his former home, where his friend and mentor was sent to the chopping block. After Raleigh's execution, Carlson raised a massive family who flourished over the next two centuries, spanning generations, becoming a pillar of the state of Virginia.

My grandfather would occasionally tell me stories about his grandfather, whom he had never met. He would tell me how his grandfather was a major in the Confederate Army who served as a personal aide de camp to General Robert E. Lee.

My grandfather's dad, who was fifty-five years his senior, would tell my grandfather how Major Carlson once owned vast land throughout northern Virginia, next to the general he served. His plans were dashed when the Union Army shattered the Confederacy and chased Lee all the way into North Carolina, just above the city named for the wild Raleigh who brought the Carlson family to the country initially. My grandfather would listen and eventually pass on stories about how devastated Lee was. He would listen to stories about how his grandfather, Major Carlson, spent hours polishing each piece of his general's brass. How impressed he was, that even in Lee's lowest moment, and darkest hour, he insisted on displaying the utmost military courtesy and bearing. He never lost control of himself, even when he knew that leading an armed rebellion against the Union would strip him of citizenship for the rest of his life. The Union confiscated Lee's beautiful plantation and accompanying land on the Potomac River, across from Washington, DC, the capital of the city against whom he declared war. The union not only confiscated his land but buried union soldiers there as if to make a point. This cemetery became Arlington and would henceforth bury the remains of the great costly wars that would loom in the future. Carlson's land was confiscated as well, but only temporarily, as a station headquarters for Union soldiers to reincorporate Confederate soldiers back into the Union and compel them to pledge their loyalty.

Carlson did not plan on remaining to learn if the Union would honor their promise. He took his family, and what few belongings he could fit into his wagon, and moved as far south and as far away from Virginia as he could. He stopped in northern Florida and replanted his roots. It was here my grandfather grew up, and it was in Florida where he returned after World War II. It was in Florida, and later Georgia, where my grandfather became a prominent civil rights attorney, never acknowledging the dark irony that his own grandfather fought in the Confederacy and even served personally the general who led the Confederacy.

I continue to sit there in front of the chairman's desk, the most uncomfortable I have felt in a while. I think of the ants I burned under my magnifying glass as a kid, when I would line up the sun's ray and the ant. I think of how the ant would just crumple and burn.

Now it is my turn. This is karma putting me under the magnifying glass and lining it with the sun and watching me simmer and sweat.

The chairman clears his throat once more, and in his deep voice, sighs out loud.

"You know, Carlson, I am truly happy that your grandfather is not alive and here to see your behavior. What would he think? You know I used to watch your grandfather argue cases, and I watched more than one of his cases on the bench!" He clears his throat again, and I look up to see his eyes burning into me as he continues, "your grandfather was the one who inspired my career in this great noble profession. When I grew up, black people had no opportunities, no respect. It was not uncommon to walk down the street and hear taunts. It was not uncommon to be verbally threatened for merely uttering a word to a young white lady. Injustice was everywhere, but it was your grandfather who taught me to *seek* justice!" The deacon in him surfaces, as he somewhat thunders the word *seek* as though he is preaching to a parish. "Your grandfather weathered a depression. After that, your grandfather went, and voluntarily, I might add, inserted himself in one of the most gruesome battles of the European theater. Your grandfather faced and helped decimate a cancer so evil and vile that its darkness had gripped the entire world! Then he came over here and shook the very foundations of the one of the most prominent and evil traditions of his own country, the institution of societal racism!" By now, his voice is thundering, and he begins to assume more of his role as a deacon, even more than a chief justice.

"In short, sir, your grandfather stared down hopelessness during the Depression, he later stared down evil in Europe, and then he stared down injustice in his own country! Now, sir, I ask you! What have you done? What are you staring down?"

For once, I am rendered silent. I suppose he is right. I did a few tours in Afghanistan, but nothing like World War II. The economy sucks, and I cannot find a job, but I have family upon which to fall back. I am silent.

"I guess you need some help! I asked you a question, and you have nothing! I inventoried all the hurdles your grandfather stared down and then asked you what you have stared down. Because you do not realize your hurdle, you cannot defeat it. So, allow me to assist! You are staring down you! In some ways this could be more difficult than those hurdles your grandfather handled because these are your own personal demons holding you captive. However, your decision to fight it is completely up to you! Your grandfather really had no choice with the Depression, racism, etc. It was just there! You choose to feel sorry for yourself. You choose to use the bottle as a medication and solution for everything. Don't think for a minute that the pack of breath mints you swallowed before entering this office shields the smell of alcohol on you, son! It does not! Now, I cannot decide for you whether or not you choose to confront these demons. However, you will answer for these inexcusable comments. I am scheduling a hearing for you to determine your ethical and character fitness to belong to the Georgia state bar and to continue as a practicing member of this noble profession for which you have lately shown complete disdain! I would suggest in the strongest of terms that you have readily available an explanation as to what possessed you to say such a thing and what you are doing to remedy this grotesque problem! I have nothing more for you, unless you have any questions!"

I sit there stunned and in silence. The whole time, I could not wait until the moment that I could bolt out of there; now I cannot move. The chief justice broke me down, made me question my own self-worth. He continues to stare at me, except now I stare back. If it were anyone else, including family, I would start punching walls, and throwing things, and even attacking he or she who had the audacity to confront me. This time, however, I am too scared, too mentally and emotionally broken down. My rage is quelled by my spiritual wounds but is still there, only suppressed, and stuffed down, until such a time that it would manifest itself in an even uglier fashion. I had to stuff my anger many times as a junior officer in the army, and it always just ate at me. Rage, like lust or hunger, must be immediately satisfied. Trying to suppress it only damages its holder that much more.

Loire Valley, France, late 1942

Anso was now numb to her new life that was no longer so new. Subconsciously, she had accepted that this was to be her reality indefinitely, but consciously, she rebelled and hated every aspect of this reality. In the past year she had lost her two best friends. She missed Genevieve so much. She felt guilty about not missing Josephine as much as her soul mate Genevieve. Although she loved Josephine, and missed her so much, Anso and Genevieve shared a bond. They shared a bond in their love for animals, the fact that they alone had to care for a disabled sibling. They shared a love for life, a disdain for phoniness, and a grit that permitted them to enjoy such life, even in its worse state. Now, here it was, life's worst conditions, and Genevieve was gone.

The Germans were now monopolizing stores and tabacs, in order to prioritize products accordingly, and rationing the leftovers to the French, who were forbidden on certain days from even entering the establishments. Proprietors still could keep their businesses, unless it was learned that they were Jewish, but each store was overseen by a squad sergeant who reported to a captain who, in turn, reported inventory to Captain Strobel. As the war effort grew, so did the need for resources to replenish the front line. Now Germany had drawn two massive giants into the conflict, Soviet Russia and the United States, and these two enemies would prove much more resilient than the smaller Euro countries over whom they effortlessly rolled. The added anxiety of the mounting need for resources, along with the mounting casualties, was now viciously handed down to the occupied French.

Meanwhile, Anso worried about her father. Their shop was slowly being choked, as people grew less concerned about framing pictures and more concerned about their limiting budgets, as a result of the Germans rationing. Her worry, accompanied by her helplessness to think of a remedy, enraged her more.

Rage is an uncontrollable impulse. Like a storm, it needs to be avoided or prepared for prior to its hitting the shore. Once it hits the land, anything in its wake is helpless. Rage works in the same manner over us. If we fail to rationalize our anger, it festers and then explodes into uncontrollable destruction.

Anso's rage finally overtook her when she was walking down the street to run errands for her mother. She only happened to see one of the Nazis going over a list of inventory in Mademoiselle Theroux's tabac. She missed the freedom of being able to casually waltz into a tabac and sit among the smokers reading their news-papers, arguing about issues that seemed mundane and stupid to-day but spurned animated chatter back then. Her mind suddenly exploded. That one sight ignited a hundred simultaneous visions of the numerous injustices these devils had inflicted. Stream of sweat formed on her scalp, and her breathing raced almost out of control as her mind went in a thousand directions. Visions of Josephine hanging from a beam in a factory, visions of her final, desperate lonely moments prior to hanging herself, visions of Genevieve's mother going insane, visions of Adrienne being loaded on the truck, visions of Genevieve being gunned down like an animal, all exploded in her mind. This was it! She was no longer going to take this lying down. She focused on the tabac. It was time to make a stand and this instant. She understood the finality of the conse-quence for disobeying the Germans. It began to sink in, and her stomach felt queasy, and her knees shook as she walked toward the tabac. Her heart felt as it would explode out of her chest as she opened the door and took a step in what was to be a certain death. She got her breathing under control and tried to harness her vision to focus only on Mademoiselle Theroux and block out the widened eyed looks on the Germans faces, surprised to see a young woman so brazenly disobeying.

"Salut! Mademoiselle!" Anso declared, trying best to keep her voice cracking under the heavy fear that was taking physical effect on her. She approached the counter and now could not help to notice the German soldiers sitting around the bistro tables, eyes brightened, and calmly, quietly studying her with curious gaze of a professor grading a student's paper.

Theroux slowly stepped up to her counter, visibly confused and frightened. She looked at the soldier studying the inventory who now had an equally confused look on his face, as she stared at her.

"Anso, what are you doing? Are you crazy? You know you cannot be in here!" Theroux whispered. Anso was momentarily amused by her whispering, as though nobody had noticed Anso's blatant defiance.

"A pack of cigarettes please!" Anso requested, pretending to have not even heard Theroux.

"Excuse me, ma'am!" the German soldier interrupted as he approached Anso's side, staring coldly at her. "Perhaps you were confused; weekdays are closed to the general public. The general public will be generously rationed their products at the end of the week!" the soldier said with a smile on his face, as though he were handing out charity to the poor.

"You have no right to ration shit! This is Theroux's tabac! You have no right to be here, you arrogant ass!" Anso screamed out, her mouth but inches away from the German's nose. Anso was so numb from the adrenaline-induced dopamine pumping through her she failed to notice Theroux nearly collapse from shock. The smile on the German's face quickly disappeared, and his face became rigid and displayed a slight annoyance. He stiffened up, locking his arms behind his back with a look on his face as though he had just been challenged. His calm and overtly professional demeanor when flustered was identical to those of Engel when he was annoyed.

"Jesus Christ! Are these robots all the same!" Anso thought to herself. She stood her ground, but her knees began to weaken; the butterflies in her stomach and her racing heart were about to overtake her. She knew she was destined for prison. She had to remain strong; she had to fight! She could not just let these bullies go unchallenged after they took from her so much, her friends, her farm, her life as she had known it for twenty years. The Germans who were sitting around enjoying their coffee and cigarettes now were extinguishing their smokes and slowly rising from the table to assist their fellow soldier. Anso could not help but to turn around and look at the Germans coming toward her. Out of corner of her eye, she saw one of the Germans motion for the rest to resume their seats, and they complied.

He then walked up behind Anso, and he motioned for the soldier confronting her to back away, and he did. Anso spun around and was facing the corporal who had purchased the frame from her shop.

"Ma'am, I think you should walk out this minute, and I promise you this will be forgotten! No consequence will be pursued, and we all forget your"—he paused and swallowed—"indiscretions."

Anso was trying desperately to muster saliva in her mouth, to spit in his face. Her mouth and throat were so dry from fear. She visualized spittle dripping down his face, but she could produce nothing. She tried to say something but could muster no such words. Her throat hurt as she tried to block the dam that held back her tears, tears of anger, and tears of fear. Her visible shaken state invoked passion in the corporal, and he pulled her closer.

"Don't worry! This war will be over one day, and we will be out of your city. But for now, play the game." He then pushed away and winked at her. He opened up the door to the tabac and motioned for her to leave, and she complied dutifully. She slowly walked out the door, humbled and defeated. She shuddered as she heard the door slam behind her. She had failed. She was not going to prison, and she failed to make her forceful statement. She collapsed onto the nearest park, her shoulders dropped, and she began to cry uncontrollably.

"Je suis desolee, ma ami!! I am so sorry, my friend!" she uttered to Genevieve, Adrienne, and Josephine, the girls she always vehemently protected. "I was a coward in front of the enemy! I am sorry!" Her long, shameful walk back to her apartment seemed to be an eternity. It was her own walk of shame. She had failed the gang of girls she had spent her short life protecting.

Her torment at her failed stand against the Nazis was not yet over. As she entered her home, she was greeted with a cold stare from her usually loving father.

"Are you out of your mind, Anso!?"

Anso stood there stunned in silence, shocked from the unexpected question.

"Don't stand there as though you have no goddamn idea what I am talking about! The whole town is already talking about the childish scene you threw at Mademoiselle Theroux's tabac! I suppose it is never going to sink in, is it!?"

If her surprise was not enough, Anso suffered an alarming, jarring slap by her father.

"What are you doing? What the hell are you trying to do!" He beamed, so uncharacteristic of the soft-spoken artist. "You openly challenged the authority!" Anso could not control herself.

"Does nobody want to challenge these people? Am I the only one who wants to fight? Are you that much of a coward?" she scolded her father. She instantly regretted. Once more, she charged her gentle father with cowardice, simply for exercising pragmatism and realizing that it was no use to attempt to face such a gargantuan, monstrous force that had squeezed its grip around her city and around her country. Yet she was so angry. The rage would not subside, nor does it ever. It only continues to fester. She could not get the fantastical image from her mind, of taking a knife and gutting those Germans she encountered in Mademoiselle Theroux's tabac. She felt betrayed that she was the only one angry about this. She felt shunned that she was the only one who wanted to rebel, to fight. She was devastated that at such a time, she was the one everyone thought of as the crazy one, when this should have been a time to rally up and collectively fight, even at the expense of their existence.

She did not know what to do. She ran out of her apartment, frustrated. She felt confined and suffocated in her home and now in her own city. She could no longer go to her favorite park because now it was fenced off. Everywhere and everything was now off limits.

She sat at a local café near the park, as close to her favorite spot as she could, and began to tear up once again. She looked out over to the river where she once smoked with her friends. She tried in vain to ignore the harsh chain-barbwire fence that separated her from her from her once sanctuary. As she sat there, plunged into hopelessness, she looked up, and through her teary, blurred eyes, she saw Minou approach her. This time the little dog was not shy or scared. He walked up to her without hesitation, and slightly kissed her, and licked her a few times, before he turned around and began sniffing around the café bistro. Anso looked on with affection. It was such a pleasant break from the hellish reality of her current life. Animals provided a break from the darkness of humanity. They only killed what they needed to eat or defend their home. Animals like Engel or Strobel did not exist, beings whose sole existence thrived and fed on cruelty. Why could human beings not be like these animals? she wondered. The dog stopped and looked up at her. Anso smiled and looked into the dog's big black but tender eyes. They made a connection. She smiled again as the dog tilted his head in a sign of affection and newfound friendship.

Anso saw the dog jerk spastically. His eyes suddenly widened as though alert and scared. Anso saw the huge patch of blood explode from the dog's side, before the rocking sound of the gunshot startled her. Then the dog's eyes were no longer tender and connecting but still and lifeless. Minou took two or three more painstaking steps and shook violently before crumpling there at Anso's feet. She looked down the street, where Captain Strobel was still aiming a smoking pistol. Captain Strobel lowered the pistol and handed it back to his accompanying soldier, nodding in approval. The one thing in this new, hideous life that made Anso's life livable the Germans had managed to take away, along with everything else, and most likely life itself, in time.

Atlanta, Georgia, Present Day

"How many times have I warned you about staying off of that Facebook!" I hear my mother gloat. I think she is actually happy about my firing, and subsequent meeting with the ethics board, as a personal vindication that I spend too much time voicing opinions online. My mother fears Facebook as a form of omnipotent Orwellian force that perpetually monitors dissenting opinions, and it turned out that this certainly is what it is. Yet I cannot for the life of me understand her fear of it. Her constant warning and disapproval over the mere mentioning of Facebook spark from her a warning that is fitting for Khrushchev era, Iron Curtain Soviet Europe.

I feel betrayed that nobody else is angry at my treatment by the ethics committee. I feel shunned that I am the only one that thinks someone's Facebook post is their expression and that alone. I feel devastated that nobody cares about the destructive, hurtful things the apparent victim said to me, but only the perception that I may have uttered something racist. Why does nobody care about the sour economy, a president's acquiescence to radical Islam? Being in my midthirties, and being reduced to living with my mom, is humiliating beyond any degradation I have ever encountered. I am an Afghanistan veteran, a former officer, and an attorney, and this is what I have been reduced to. I know other veterans in similar situations. Those are the lucky ones. Some are flat-out homeless, and of course, my friend, Mark, who simply ended it. I feel shunned in a society in which I am meant to thrive. In short, I feel like a young Anso did in 1942 Loire Valley.

Four

REDEMPTION

Redemption. Redemption is the act of pulling oneself up out of disgrace. Some acts are so repugnant, they may never be redeemed. Redemption is the making and offering of reparation for past actions or words or any other harmful deed.

Loire Valley, France

Shooting those two Germans she encountered in the tabac became a dark obsession that gnawed upon Anso's mind. Absentia anything else to think about, among an abysmal boredom resulting from the lack of business, school, and now her closest friends, her mind could entertain little else. After so long, she even tried to flush the image from her mind of that smiling jerk with a bleeding hole in his head, or blood gurgling out of his mouth, as she plunged a knife into his stomach. Her fantastical image she entertained in order to maintain her sanity and stave off the helpless feeling, had now taken her hostage, much in the same manner as did Major Engel's Wehrmacht sturm unit that occupied her city .

She mulled about her father's store. She was completely alone. Everyone thought she was crazy for having wanted to fight. All her life, she was somewhat of an outcast. Even as Josephine told her before she had committed suicide, the boys would have liked her, but her attitude. Before the occupation, she had the luxury of saying,

"To hell with them anyway!" Her life was complete without the extra attention that seemed to enthrall young Josephine. Anso could always retreat to the country, amid the animals she loved so much, the Benoit family. But now all of that was gone, and she was stuck with the family, and city people that rejected her as crazy. She hated the Germans, and now she hated the hapless citizens who just seemed to sit back and take it. God, how she missed Genevieve! It had been weeks now since those monsters took Adrienne and then gunned down Genevieve and her mother.

As she mulled about the shop, trying to extinguish the image of that German soldier, she heard the door open. Standing there was the German corporal she had encountered at the tabac and who had ordered her out. Seeing the person she had just been imagining butchered sent Anso into a silent shock. This was the corporal who not only had ordered her out of the tabac but had commissioned her father to build a frame for that disgusting Hitler portrait now hanging in the hotel de ville.

Before Anso could so much as utter anything, the corporal spoke first.

"I know you don't like us. And I also know that you don't trust me. But listen when I tell you this. My unit has recommenced going through the hospital records. A few weeks ago, they were in the Bs and learned about Adrienne Benoit's condition..."

He did not have to finish. Anso's body became numb. Now they were in the Cs. Chevalier! They were coming for little Thomas! They were coming to take him away and kill him for his limitations! She collapsed and fell to the floor. Her toughness was now depleted. She had to concede; she was completely helpless. First, she had to watch them rape and drive Josephine to suicide; after they senselessly and brutally killed Josephine's family, then they did the same to Genevieve's family. They deprived her of the joys of everyday French life. Now they were coming to kill her little Thomas. Heaving, and unable to catch her own breath, her soul was sinking down a bottomless pit. She began to have trouble breathing; she felt the walls condense around her. The world was literally falling around her.

She then felt a hand grip her under both arms and shoulders and lift her up on her now useless feet. She began to regain feeling. Her breathing began to return. Through tear-blurred vision, she could somewhat make out the corporal's face.

"Mademoiselle, don't worry. They will not round him up until tonight after curfew lockdown. In the meantime, I know where we can take him, where they will never find him. It is still morning, and we have time to move him out of the city. With me, you will not need permission from the captain to leave the city parameters," the corporal said in a gentle voice. It was the first time Anso could remember any of these soldiers sounding human and not robotic. She buried her face in his shoulder and cried. For the first time, someone acknowledged that she was not crazy for hating the madness coalescing around her.

ATLANTA, GEORGIA

Ten thirty in the morning, and I am stirring about. I am groggy and still tired. I hear my mother stomping about downstairs. She calls up to me. I hate it. I miss my life, my privacy. I wish I could stay drunk. Today, I have a trip to make. I must go to Tallahassee to help my grandmother with her estate planning. It pains me to think that at ninety, she may not be around too much longer. Looking at her, one would never believe she was ninety. She still looks and has the energy of most people in their sixties.

My grandmother took me to France for the first time at a very young age. My grandparents flew us into Paris, and I marveled at the age-old buildings, so different from the rapid sprawling, hastily constructed shopping centers that slowly encroached upon the rural land of Gwinnett I knew when I was younger. Later, when I was a troublesome teen, and temporarily kicked out of my house after repetitive run-ins with the law, my grandmother took me in. I finished high school living with my grandparents. My grandparents lived on the same farm in Bradfordville, Florida, that a young Vic Carlson had purchased upon his return from the war, with his new wife, Anso Chevalier Carlson.

I finally get out of bed, dress, and slowly make it down the stairs. My mother is chipper and on her fourth cup of coffee, watching her twenty-four-hour, round-the-clock, news cycle.

"Well, good morning! Are you going to be ready to go soon?"

"I think so," I reply, not looking at her but reaching for some coffee before I can shake off the grogginess of the previous evening.

"Your show is about to come on," she reminds me.

"I know," I mumble as I pour my coffee. Television has become a companion almost as important as the internet in my now long exodus from employment of usefulness. Even back when I practiced law and had a job, I always enjoyed watching Dr. Frenz on CNN. He is an Ivy League professor of economics and international affairs. He clearly has an Eastern European background, by his accent.

His show, *Global Report*, discusses all the issues plaguing the world, be they economic, civil strife, or cultural. I used to always watch him back in my former life. Today, his show acts as my now one link to my former life, when I was independent, when I was free.

"I cannot believe you had a chance to meet Dr. Frenz, and you didn't want to!" my mom comments. I have only heard that a million damn times.

"You and your wife were touring the CNN center in downtown. Yes, that's right. Your friend worked there and was able to take you on a tour they did not even give the tourists, and you had the chance to meet Karl Frenz."

"Yes, goddamnit!" I interrupt. "I know! I did not want to meet the great Karl Frenz Jr.!"

My old friend from my old unit in Afghanistan was a signal officer. We left the army around the same time. His computer skills landed him a good job at CNN, where he oversaw the team that put CNN terminal sets throughout the airports. He traveled often and visited the CNN headquarters with equal frequency. Many times, he would take me through the headquarters during operating hours and newscasts. I met Anderson Cooper, Erin Burnett, and yes, even the nationally popular, well-liked, and world-renowned Karl Frenz Jr.

But even before that, I can honestly say that I knew Dr. Frenz. I knew him better than many, even my own mother, my ex, or even my friend at that time, actually knew.

⟫⟪⟫⟪

NICE, FRANCE, MEDITERRANEAN COAST, 1942

Anso was surprised and impressed with how sharp the young corporal proved himself to be. She spent the day riding shotgun in the German truck; the corporal was driving. They had Thomas hidden the back as they transported him out of the city and on a long trip to the southeastern, Mediterranean part of France that was run by the Italians' Mussolini Fascist government, Germany's weak ally. While Italy was an ally, they were not as ideological, and not as eager to rid the world of Jewish, or handicapped, nor eager for the perfect race, as was Hitler's Germany. The corporal told the guards at the city fence that Anso was chosen to help him with his duties. The corporal was lower ranking, but because he was the personal assistant and driver for Major Engel, rarely was he ever questioned by higher-ranking noncommissioned officers within the sturm. Major Engel was off to Berlin to attend a Nazi conference, by the Wehrmacht Commanding General, for his quarterly brief on the occupied civilians, threats of uprisings, and confiscation of "undesirables." In Major Engel's absence, the corporal was a relatively free and went about his day, under the assumption that he was enacting the priorities of Engel.

This also meant that the dreaded, sadistic Captain Strobel now was the administrative kommandant of the city. Engel was evil but reasonable. Strobel was just depraved and masochistic. While many Germans tolerated being in the Nazi army simply for convenience of belonging to a powerful force, Strobel was suited for the Nazi party and their historic cruelty.

Life always surprises. Anso always mocked religion. Most of her disdain was merely natural rebellion to a small city that was stoically Catholic. The catastrophic events of the past two years did nothing to solidify any belief, no matter how diminished, of a gentle higher power. Nonetheless, a young Anso had to admit that there did exist an external plan, and this plan often unfolded itself in the most inappropriately ironic manner. Never did she expect to be so thankful to be riding with a uniformed member of the Wehrmacht, one whom she wanted to kill only shortly prior, at that.

Anso had forgotten how much she missed the warmer climate of the southern Mediterranean coast of France. They drove down through the Haute Garonne region of central-southern France. She thought about her cousin in Brive. When they approached the Mediterranean region just above Touloun, she began to think about Laurent and Josephine. Laurent's family was from Touloun. The people were darker, less formal. Anso had forgotten how she longed for this place. The weather was warmer on the Mediterranean cities of Touloun and Marseilles, and the sun usually always shined, unlike the constant overcast gray skies of northern and central France.

They approached the small enclave apartment of Anso's mother's brother, an equally outspoken Charles. Anso could not stop taking in the warm, moist air and palm trees of the coastal, semi-Italian-influenced city. Anso was impressed with the tender care with which the German corporal helped a frightened Thomas out of the back of his truck. She knew it had to be tough for a kid harboring mental disabilities to hide in the back of a truck for hundreds of kilometers. Uncle Charles stood out on the balcony of their second-story apartment, watching the corporal help little Thomas up the old staircase.

Uncle Charles opened the door in his usual smiling, inviting manner. He kissed Anso on both cheeks!

"Como cava?" as was his usual, soft greeting. Uncle Charles had an almost bipolar personality, where he could be the loving southern European in one instance and impulsive and temperamental the next second. After greeting Anso, and manually assisting young Thomas to his wife, he stood up and sneered at the German corporal. Anso made a quick facial gesture, begging her uncle to cease the disrespect. Both the corporal and Anso helped young Thomas up the stairs, where he was welcomed by his cousin's family! Finally! Little Thomas would be safe. Whereas just that morning, he was facing certain death, tonight he would be in the loving company of his uncle, in one part of France that was relatively free.

Anso had always enjoyed her cousins in the south. They had a more laid-back lifestyle. Mediterranean culture, even within the same country, was different than the stiffer, formalized culture of the rest of Europe.

Anso spent a few nights with them in Nice, where she got to see her cousin, Jacques, after years of absence. Jacques was thrilled to see her, as he worried about her, being under the direct supervision of the Nazis. The Italians, Anso learned, were not quite as forceful or regimented as the Germans had been. The Italian officer running Nice was rarely found, and when he was, he was drinking wine and had not close to the professional, military demeanor that Engel displayed. The Italians still confiscated most of the domestic production for the Italian effort, and to assist the Germans, but their organization was so slack, and so easily were the Italians tempted, that occupation was not nearly the hell it was under the Nazis, and Anso felt good leaving Thomas there. In fact, Anso herself would have stayed, but for the idea of abandoning her parents to be stuck with that psycho Strobel.

While Anso stayed by the side of the corporal, nobody, French or Italian alike, dared question her about anything. Anso enjoyed the leisure meals in the choice eating establishments that she could now enjoy once again, after what seemed like an eternity. Her break and reprieve from her never-ending prison sentence under Engel's oppressive, iron-fisted rule.

Anso and the corporal even had the luxury of stopping to eat at a seaside café. Anso could not recall the last time she had been able to enjoy seafood.

"So, can I ask you a question?" Anso asked, noticing she was no longer the outspoken rebel she once was, when she felt like the world was in her grasp. Helplessness and the need for this German's mercy had taken its toll.

"Go ahead!" the corporal replied, not looking up from his plate. The corporal did not look like the other Germans. He did not share their sharp features, but had a chubbier face, and did not have the manners of the rest of the Wehrmacht. He inhaled his food and sucked down his beer.

"Why are you helping me and my family?"

The corporal paused and was stopped in his tracks. He quit chewing and took a big swallow as he stared at Anso for a moment that seemed frozen in time.

"I have a sister back home who is in a wheelchair. She is a wonderful young woman and has a bright future ahead of her. "

"Tell me about her!" Anso inquired cheerily.

The corporal stopped and smiled back at her.

"You know, that is the first time I have ever seen you smile. That is the first time I have seen you smile since I met you."

"Well, you know, these past months, probably won't go down as the highest point of joy and prosperity in French history!" Anso retorted sarcastically.

The corporal looked down ashamed, and Anso could tell he was uncomfortable and at a loss for words.

"Ha! You are good with typing words but tongue-tied when attempting to articulate them!" Anso said with a confident, victorious smile.

"Look, I think what the Nazis are doing to the disadvantaged is wrong. I am not for it."

Anso exhaled impatiently.

"Look, I don't agree with everything they are doing!" the corporal whispered over the table.

"You mean everything that *you* are doing?" Anso challenged, coldly staring at the young man, escorting her for what was a day reprieve from a never-ending nightmare.

He continued to stare at her.

"Look, judge me if you will. Trust me. You little girls are so naive, so ill informed. You French live in your own protected world. You have no idea how evil the alternative is. You have no idea what Stalin is like. You haven't a clue what slavery Communism is. And you have no idea what this monster is capable of. Yes, Germans are monsters too, but they are lesser of the two. You can judge me if you will," he repeated. "But trust me! We are the good guys in this war. Or at least, we are the closest things to good guys you will find. Trust me, if you are ever unfortunate enough to encounter those cannibalistic animals in Stalin's Red Army, and by Christ I hope that we do not, or that means we are dead, you will wish that you were resting under the safe umbrella provided by the Germans. But I know it's easy to judge me now!"

"I don't judge, trust me," Anso ironically replied, unaware of how judgmental she was.

"Of course you don't!" the corporal replied, pausing his lunch once more, "Jesus Christ judges me! As he will come back to judge all the living and the dead!"

"Oh wow! And you believe in God also!" Anso mockingly grinned.

The young corporal only responded by silently looking up from his plate to once more stare at her.

"Well, I mean, you see the irony in that, right?"

The corporal stopped. He finished his beer and motioned the waiter to bring him another.

"Look! I brought you and your brother here, right!"

To this, Anso had no real facetious reply. She had no stinging comment with which she could mock the ridiculousness of those matters that were held sacred by humanity, as they simultaneously committed subhuman acts. This time, for once, she was rendered completely silent. For the young corporal, as arrogant and difficult as he could be, was this time right, so right! He helped her hide and save her little Thomas from the cruel evil clutches of the jaws of the Nazi machine.

Redemption.

After a few days, Anso had to return to her city. It broke her heart to leave her cousin and leave behind the more laid-back life to which she had been accustomed most of her life, in favor of the harsh, regimented, fearful life under the Wehrmacht. The corporal had dropped her off away from the view of any potential onlooking soldiers. Anso returned to her apartment in the morning and was met by her mother and father who sobbed as they hugged her, thankful that she had been able to save her brother's life. Anso was no longer the crazy one. She was no longer the crank who ranted and railed about tolerating this horror that had gripped its city. She was now the hero who saved her brother from impending death.

Such hero status was only to last so long. That evening, a loud knock on the door thudded the tranquil peace that was now after curfew hour. Monsieur Chevalier looked confused, then scared, as the knocking continued, even louder and more forceful. He slowly and timidly went over the door to open it. Standing in the doorway, as he pushed the door wider open, was Captain Strobel and his two accompanying soldiers. Strobel was adorned in his dress uniform, sharp with swastika band; his soldiers in their coats and helmets entered the apartment with their rifles pointed, one at Mademoiselle Chevalier, and one at Anso's father. Strobel paused and then casually strolled through the threshold of the door, calmly his hands behind his back.

He cleared his throat and then spoke.

"We know you have a cripple here!" Anso could feel her rage welling up at hearing her brother referred to as merely cripple. She then remembered when Jean Luc made the same offensive error and remembered the penalty he suffered. Then her spirits sank as she remembered that he was taken away. Where to, only God knew! God! What a joke! What kind of a world was this where she felt sorry for a bully like Jean Luc. She looked at the beads of sweat forming on Strobel's forehead, partially concealed by the black bangs that hung over his forehead almost concealing those equally black, beady eyes.

"Furnish for us the cripple now. And we shall forget this"—again he cleared his throat—"this minor mistaken discrepancy."

The silence in the room was itself deafening. Anso could see her father motion as if ready to speak. She wanted to telepathically tell him to remain quiet.

"There appears to be a mistake, sir!" Monsieur Chevalier declared meekly.

"So, you are telling me that you don't have a young son named Thomas? A son who is wheelchair bound? You are to have me believe that the hospital records are then false?" Strobel sternly asked, in a perturbed voice.

"Sir, we had a son named Thomas. He died from his complications," Chevalier said.

"And what complication would that be exactly?" Strobel quietly asked as he slowly moved toward Chevalier, his nose inches from his face. "Monsieur!"

Monsieur Chevalier stood petrified. Unable to take his eyes from the intimidating gaze of Strobel, he lost notice that there was a German rifle pointed right at him not four feet away.

"I will give you one more chance, monsieur! Where. is. Thomas Chevalier? Understand, sir, that you are in disobedience to the Wehrmacht, and your punishment will be imprisonment, and then execution following the war. Do I make myself clear?"

Strobel then motioned with his eye for them to move in on Monsieur Chevalier. Anso and her mother stood in such fright; they did not even notice anyone enter their apartment. Before the two accompanying soldiers could move in to seize Chevalier, they quickly spun around and reaffixed their rifles on the man pointing a rifle at the head of Strobel. Strobel, immediately sensing that someone was behind him, stood upright, and slowly turned around, as though positive his assailant would not fire.

———◦《◎》◦———

TALLAHASSEE, FLORIDA, 2015

I look forward to seeing my cousins. Ever since my firing and subsequent unemployment, I had avoided them. I am now the unemployed one in the family. I am now the one whom everyone whispers about at dinner. As bad as it seems, I hate hearing how great everyone is doing, while I am so miserable. I am often reminded about how I was once the one who was doing the best among the cousins. Now I am the dependent. Nevertheless, it is always good to see them again. It is always good to head down to Florida, even if it is the panhandle. Of all my most cherished childhood memories, those that stand out the most are the memories spent with my cousins in that huge farm in Tallahassee.

My dad was the black sheep of the family. His eternal conflict with my grandfather never failed to be the topic of conversation anytime I encountered anyone who knew both my father and the stern judge. My father moved us to Atlanta when I was barely six months old. Nevertheless, twice yearly, we made the trip down to visit my cousins and Aunt Genny, Uncle Thomas, and Aunt Josie. Aunt Genny and Uncle Thomas had kids who became my best friends each summer that I would spend in Tallahassee.

While Aunt Josie was my aunt, and my dad's youngest sister, I always considered her more of a cousin, especially as I grew older. Born in the midsixties, when her oldest brother, my father, was graduating from high school, she was on the very tail end of the baby boomer generation. She was a baby boomer who had never really experienced the sixties, the Vietnam War, or the civil rights movement that spawned her generation. She took race for granted, only because she was too young to remember people being treated like animals as they could not drink or piss where white people could. She was just arriving into womanhood in the eighties during a an era, when the older members of her generation were clinging to their idealistic identities, in an age that saw the assassination of John Lennon, the physical unraveling of Muhammad Ali, sports and civil rights icon. She was embracing a consumer culture and lived guilt free in a world that her generation had promised themselves to deny and reject but embraced nonetheless, as they purchased multiple houses, cars, and appliances. Aunt Josie never promised that she would never trust anyone over thirty, and therefore looked forward to her thirties.

The amusing irony of my aunt's life was that she had never promised herself the carefree lifestyle she lived. She simply lived it. My aunt Josie was amused at those women who cast their scorn upon her for failing to embrace the constraining life of marriage, children, mortgage payments, and 401Ks. They happened to be the same women who years ago walked around nude and unshaven, burning their bras along with the US flag and swearing to never submit themselves to such a patriarchal, institutionalized society. Now these women teetered on the border of insanity as they carefully tried to balance the corporate careers, they relentlessly chased with the taxing duties of wiping noses and cleaning soiled asses and shuttling children from tae kwon do, to gymnastics, to violin lessons.

These women, who once swore off capitalism as evil, now built billion-dollar industries as they patronized mental therapy and pharmaceuticals once they breached that dangerous edge of sanity, if only temporarily. They turned physical fitness into a colossal corporate giant as they ordered Jane Fonda fitness tapes. These women who so despised my aunt hired personal trainers, who later became sexual affairs, and paid millions in supplemental vitamins. Meanwhile, my aunt Josie simply indulged in the occasional bag of marijuana and some cheap yoga for mental therapy, and her involvement in the fitness industry was a hike through the trails of whatever location she found herself, be it the Bavarian Alps, the Lush Hawaiian windward side, or the rainy, chilly forest of Washington State.

Her failure to marry was not for lack of interested suitors. Her striking looks, and ability to capture the attention and obsession of every boy, was about the only trait she shared with her namesake, Josephine, a young woman in the Loire Valley who mentally collapsed and ended her life decades prior. However, much to the chagrin of my grandparents, and other families in the community who had wanted their sons to date Josephine, she was bored with those who captivated the attention of every other girl. Other girls' disdain of Josie was out of jealousy for the boys' attention and rage toward her audacious indifference to their obsessive attention. Many of the families within the community equally held my aunt in contempt for her rejection of their perfect, whitewashed, crystalized versions of American perfection that were their sons. Parents of young men whose monumental feats included recruitment to play football for Alabama, and later the Pittsburgh Steelers, acceptance to Harvard, valedictorians, and even Rhoades scholarships could never comprehend why the attractive daughter of the judge and famous attorney never showed so much as marginal interest.

My education was extensive, holding a juris doctorate and having served as a commissioned officer in the army and flight school. Yet the profundity of my education was not formal but derived from the brigade of misfits that were lucky enough to win Josie's favor. These young men did not descend from good families; in fact, many did not even know their families. Yet their skills were those acquired by baptism by fire only a runaway or neglected child would know. Their academic feat was the fact that they still existed, after an abusive father or being on their own on the streets and having to figure out how to acquire food and shelter. These young men were exotic in their own way. Yet like the exotic locales that Josie once called her home, she was quickly off to another place. The world was too vast for Josie, and there was too much to explore, and too little time in which to do so. And so it was with the men in her life.

Throughout my lonely, outcast youth, I learned many lessons from them. I learned how to build a shelter, start a fire, and search for food from one guy who was once homeless after his mom abandoned him. One guy had left a band, that later became world famous, to go join the army special forces. He taught me that when confronting a much bigger opponent, you kick toward his upper thigh. The opponent will think that you are going for his crotch and will cover the jewels, while you slam his upper thigh, the one fiber joint that connects his legs to the hip, thus sending him into temporary but debilitating femur shock. I learned that when interested in a girl, don't pay her too much attention; I learned how to properly roll a joint, and a series of other everyday survival techniques.

After I joined the army, I never heard too much from her. She would only return to Tallahassee ever so periodically, and now that grandmother was arranging her wishes for her estate, she was there. None of us wanted to imagine our grandmother passing. Even though she was approaching her late nineties, she still appeared to be in her sixties. Her mind was intact, and her energy lent her to giving French lessons and doing volunteer work. She still appeared to have decades left, not mere years.

I drove into the gravel parking place in front of the old, nine-teenth-century-style, wood-shingle house. I never made it to the door before my grandmother was opening the door for me, always hearing me, my arrival betrayed by the crunch of the gravel. She always had a wonderful smile, as we kissed both cheeks, the French greeting tradition. She always had coffee and some delicatessen ready for me, where the kitchen nearly resembled a Parisian café, rich with delicatessens. Many times, it was enough to merely stand there and take in the scent of fresh, rich coffee. It was a house that had become a home to me. It was a place where I spent my teenage years.

"Why don't you come around more?" she asks me in her thick French accent.

"I will, mamoun, I promise," I always remind her.

We sit down and talk. We sip coffee, and relax.

"So, what is going on your life?" she asks.

"Oh, you know. Just juggling opportunities. Trying to see which job I want to take," I lie. I do not want meme to see me in this condition, nor worry about my hopeless situation.

"Listen! Honeypot. You will find something. You are smart!" she reassures and winks, nonverbally telling me that she knows I am full of shit but wants to reassure me nonetheless.

"Is Aunt Josie back from Oregon?" I ask, looking around.

"Oh yes! She is in town. But she is out and about! You know her—she never hangs around anywhere for too long. Well, are we ready to go?" she asks me cheerily. "On a vas?"

I had agreed to take her to the Presbyterian church, where she went to socialize.

"Mamoun, why do you go to church? You never liked religion," I ask while driving and staring over the top of the steering wheel.

"Well, I don't attend services. I only go to socialize. It is the only place where I can find people my own age. You know, when people are young, nobody goes to church, but when they see the end around the corner, they start crowding into church just in case." She rolls her eyes.

Vividly, I remember her encountering outpouring religious figures, who swarmed the American South, putting salesmen to shame with their massive recruiting efforts.

"Ma'am, do you have a personal relationship with Jesus Christ?" they would ask her in their charming, polite, Southern accent.

"Oh, I don't know that I have a strong personal relationship with very many!" she replied, as the churchgoer jumped back, taken by her strong French accent, accompanied by her seeming irreverence.

"Well, you know God sent his only son, our great Lord Jesus Christ, whom I take as my savior, to save humankind."

"Well, I don't think humankind is that much worth it. And for somebody to send their only son? That sounds selfish to me! I would never send my own children; why doesn't he go himself?"

"Well, ma'am, he came! He came in the form of his son!" the

poor man tried uselessly to explain, only to see my grandmother look at him out of the corner of her rolled eyes and a skeptical look.

"God loved us so much. After all, he made us in his own image!" he proclaimed, as though he were telling the world that he won the lottery.

"Well, if he made people in his image, then he must not be that impressive! You know people are the worst form of life on this planet. Listen, you see these little animals. They would never hurt another human being, the way that people hurt each other," my grandmother lectured.

"Ma'am, I assure you, a few days in the jungle, or in the cage of a lion, you may readjust."

"Sure, they will kill people, or each other, but to eat, for necessity. But no other living thing kills, maims, or tortures simply for the act of inflicting pain."

"Well, ma'am, that is because we have been corrupted by the temptation of the devil, Satan, the prince of all darkness and destruction."

"Oh, pffff!!" was my grandmother's only reply as she waved her hand dismissively.

It was hopeless. It was well-known, throughout the community, Anso Chevalier Carlson, the judge's wife, held contempt for not only religion but for the depraved humanity who insisted on it. While my grandfather would awaken at six each Sunday morning to attend Anglican services, his wife would stay home.

Only later would I hear the stories of the brutal regime that overtook the beautiful old city where I had spent many a summer in my adolescence and how this regime and their casual cruelty would rob my grandmother of any belief in the good of humanity. Now, after many decades and the bitterness having worn off like rust, it only manifested itself in a humorous sarcasm, directed at those young Americans who took optimism far too seriously. Today, everyone at the church knows that attempting to persuade someone who socializes at church to actually attend a service is futile. She is there to comingle with people her age. Consideration for her using the church as her own personal night club does exist, as my grandmother gives beginner and advanced French classes. The church provides free classes to the local kids in the impoverished subdivisions and free tutoring to high school and Florida State students who are members of the parish.

"Only Americans are this religious!" my grandmother continues.

"Well, there is this place called the Middle East. I have been there a time or two, ya know. They only blast this music out that sounds like cats being tortured, and everyone must immediately drop to their knees and stick their butt in the air. I might say they have us beat in religion."

I shar my grandmother's disdain of religion. Growing up Catholic, knowing a kid abused by a priest, seeing their coverup, and then seeing what led up to and unfolded after 9/11, I am of a generation of people who shunned faith more and more.

"I tell you, this place is not France!" she continues. And here we go again.

I sometimes wonder if Victor Carlson gagged and kidnapped my grandmother to smuggle her over here. It would be my only explanation for my grandmother's six-decade disapproval of her now-not-so-new, adopted country.

"You promise me that no matter what happens, promise me that you will not turn out like these fat, lazy Americans!" she pleads in her thick accent.

"Well, you know, not every American is this fat, gruesome slob; there are some clean-cut, fit, well-dressed Americans, you know!" But fate that day is not on my side. Just as I utter that, a group of black kids stroll out of a video game store, holding their plastic bags with one hand and with the other, holding up their jeans by the crotch, as their pants sag a foot below their white-clothed ass. They hobble out as though something is in their pants. They could not have tried to appear more slovenly.

"Oh, look at that! You would never see that in Paris!" my grandmother comments.

"Not everybody!" I insist as we continued down Thomasville Highway.

Then we pass a Little John's Pizza, where a redneck hobbles out, almost in the same manner as the kids a block back. He could not have been less than three hundred pounds, multiple chins, and his belly hanging out of a black AC/DC shirt. Thankfully he is not moving fast, for his poor wife, who seems only fifty pounds lighter, struggles to keep up as she maneuvered out the door, holding one kid, and also pushing a stroller, and another one in tow.

"Oh, look at that!" she again comments. She is not going to be redundant, for it does not take a shrink to figure out what she is thinking.

Finally, we are downtown, where Thomasville and Meridian Road meet. As we pull around the building to park, three young guys, decked out in black, dyed black hair, and black mascara and lipstick are hanging out behind a building smoking weed.

"I tell you, I am glad you did not turn out to be like these Americans," she comments, never missing a chance to show how France is so much superior to the US.

She helps herself out of the car and briskly walks past, ignoring the Goth pot smokers, and straight to the church. I lock up the car and follow behind her. As we enter the premises, I se Aunt Josie, light up, smile, and wave, as she moves toward us.

Both Aunt Josie and I know some of the parishioners as sometimes my grandmother would drag us to church to assist and help teach her French classes. While each one of her children and grandchildren spent at least two summers in France, with her cousins' families, only Josie and I really keep up with the language and make it a point to return regularly.

"Hey there, GI Joe!" Aunt Josie knows I hate that. "Or I am sorry, Mr. Johnny Cochran!"

"You know, Josie, there are other attorneys besides that guy! He has been dead, you know! I mean, how about comparing me to Atticus Finch!"

"Oh, Christ! Just like your grandpa! So self-righteous. I think Grandpa even dressed himself like Atticus Finch!"

"Oh, wow! You know who Atticus Finch is! Impressive! So, when on the Kardashians did they discuss him, and pray tell, what context?"

My aunt only responds with a roll of her eyes and a middle finger.

"Flipping people off at church! Show that class!"

"Oh! I am glad to see you're starting to hold something sacred! So, what was her name, and how did she get you to go to church! Oh, I forgot! All Latin girls go to church!"

"Classy, respectful, and racist! Good deal!"

"Yep, ole Vic Carlson would be proud!" she responds to my accusation.

"You mean, he did not envision us divorced, showing up to church stoned, cursing, and flipping off each other!" I say, and we both laugh. It is good to see her again. While I applaud the freedom her apathy affords her, I do miss seeing her more often.

"You know, it is amazing!" she whispers to me, changing the subject. "All these old people who are being wheeled in here, on oxygen. Bless their hearts. Some of them look like they are about 90 percent in the grave."

"Josie!" I almost yell, taken aback at her irreverence.

"Chill! I am just making a point! I mean look in their eyes. Bless their hearts, they are tough, but their eyes, you can tell, they are ready to go. They can barely move. And here is my mom, five to ten years older than all of them, just bouncing around the place."

Toward the end of the afternoon, we head back to the farm, and more of the cousins, as well as my parents and brother, who begin to roll in. I always missed the big family gatherings, where we turned the old living room into a lounge, my grandmother would put on a phonograph record, and drank wine into the night. Aunt Genny's kids, who are just a few years my junior, Phillip and Will, are there. Along with my brother, the four cousins are all separated by a year, where I am the oldest; then Phillip is a year younger. My brother, Rubin, is a year younger than Phillip, and Will is the youngest.

Will is the only one of the cousins who resembles the Carlson family, and coincidentally, he was named for the family's first American pioneer to brave the wilderness and colonies. And like William Carlson, centuries before, his vast success originated by his fortunate associations. Where William Carlson benefitted greatly from his association with Sir Walter Raleigh, young Will formed an early association with a tech giant, whose company had recently been bought out by Google.

While Phillip did not enjoy quite the financial success of his younger brother, he had a well-paying job as an IT tech. He took a two-year sabbatical to tour Europe, and it is there he met his beautiful Swedish wife, with whom he has two very blond, good-looking kids.

I am the only one who is not doing well in the family. It is one of the main reasons I remain aloof. I am not like my aunt Josie. My failure at success had crippled me mentally and spiritually. I am just like my dad, as my mother revels in reminding me, a whip she loves to wield as I am already down.

I hate us growing apart. As children, my brother and I would spend the summers at this big old house, with my cousins. Thomas, who we called Uncle Keys because he was the Key West lawyer, only recently had a child with his beautiful, wife, who is a famed Israeli model and athlete.

The cousins and their families begin filtering into the old farm. Phillip's wife's Swedish family is in town for the occasion. They are always impressed at the late festivities and boisterousness of the family of a respected late judge who hailed from a protestant, Anglican family.

"It seems as though there is always a party here!" Maria's mother comments.

Everyone is here for the occasion. My grandmother is turning 91. At her age, she is in the best shape of anybody I know twenty years her junior.

I step out on the porch. Nighttime seems to be the only time in the panhandle where I am not constantly sweating, and the intense humidity actually makes for a pleasant evening. I stare off in the darkness, wondering how many more of these soirees life will grant us. Although the whole purpose of my visit is to generate a will, my grandmother's mortality is something I am not prepared to face.

Standing outside, I become suddenly reminded and aware of all the problems facing me back in Atlanta. I wish for anything that will break this enslaving train of thought. We should be careful what we wish for.

My aunt Genny receives a call.

"Hello!" She pauses. "This is she." Then this is followed by a longer pause.

"Oh, wow! Uhm, sure! Please! Come on over!" she slowly utters, while sounding somewhat confused as she pushes the button on her phone.

She looks up with a combined look of shock and excitement

"Hey, everybody! Dr. Frenz on CNN is coming over!"

"Who the hell is that?"' is one response.

"You mean Karl Frenz, the guy on CNN?" one of the Swedish people asks.

How I cringed that a Swede knows who Dr. Frenz on CNN is and not any Americans.

"What the hell does he want?" is one of my cousin's responses.

"Yes, Dr, Frenz. You know he hosts global reports on CNN every week" is my aggravated response. I have often enjoyed his show. I enjoy his take on issues plaguing the world, of which I have often traveled and know so much.

"That is awesome!" exclaims Uncle Keys. I am sure that Uncle Keys knows who Frenz is, as we have spent mornings before tennis matches watching his program and drinking coffee, back when I interned with his office while living in Key West. That was back before I knew who Karl Frenz Tr. truly was. That was back before I knew just how intertwined he is in our family, even unbeknownst to the great professor.

"He wants to see you, Mom" is Aunt Genny's response.

The Visiting Professor

My heart begins to instantly race. I know what this means. It does not take long for the excitement to dissipate, and soon enough, everyone is back to drinking, talking, and enjoying the fire. I sit there and fret. I try to readjust fire. I try to recalibrate my obsessive anxiety with my real career-ending problems facing me at home. I try, but the storm that is calmly brewing is going unnoticed among everyone else in this room.

Then I hear the crackling of a car going over the gravel, followed by a knock. My aunt jumps up toward the door, and I get up to follow. I know this was going to be bad. My aunt opens the door before I can get to it; there he is standing. The great doctor Frenz Jr., whom everyone knows as CNN's professor. He looks much younger than his sixty years would have betrayed. Tan, oily skin, gray, curly hair, but well-kept, and nurtured, give him the appearance of one who takes care of himself, eats well and in moderation, and dresses well.

His flashes a curt smile, indicating a less-than-thrilled look. He enters the place with an entitled sense, as I imagine he feels wherever he goes.

I immediately block his way.

"Dr. Frenz, sir!" I loudly address him.

"Hi!" he greets in a commanding voice.

"You cannot come in here!" I order.

"Wait! We told him to. We invited him!"

"No, you don't know why is here!" I warn.

"Son! We are okay, seriously!" Dr. Frenz assures me.

"No, shitbag! You do not just waltz in here, as though this is your set! It is not! You are not filming another version of your goddamn show!" I shove back.

He stands up closer to my face, flashing a smug grin, as if to ask, "Who in the hell are you, and how dare you?"

I cannot explain what exactly happened, how, or even in what order. I do not feel my fists swing, not even feel them connect with Frenz's gut. I do remember his handlers rushing to grab me and sort of remember them pulling me down. Really, I just remember going down slowly. I do not see my family's reaction, but hear gasps. From whom they emitted, I cannot say; maybe it was Aunt Genny, or maybe it was my mother. I feel and sense the intense and negative energy that now densifies the room. Humans possess a sixth sense that overrides all our other five senses that simply connect us on the surface. I cannot see my mother but can feel her hurt. I cannot hear my father, nor know if he even says anything, but can feel his disappointment in my internal being.

By the time I am cuffed and in the police car, I feel in sanctum. I am protected from that dreadful energy that overhung my being since my firing and subsequent unemployment. Cuffed and in this police car, I am safe among officers who were unaware of the failure I have become. I look up and see the officer at the door, speaking with my aunt, who still seems to be in utter shock. The officer takes copious notes as he occasionally peers back at me. Finally, I see my grandmother come to the door with a devastated look on her face as she worriedly looks out toward the car. I was her favorite, the one in the police car. Thankfully I am shielded by the darkness of the cab, and she is the one rendered visible by the headlights and flashing blue and red lights. Devastated, I wish the situation were reversed, and I could not see her.

My grandmother and I have more in common than our longing for our French culture that defines us and sets us apart from our current culture to which we both feel imprisoned. We are both engulfed in a moment we dread, but knew was coming. My moment is watching the officer close his notepad and walk toward the car. I am hoping he is going to take me downtown and book me, but I know I am in for no such luck.

"Okay, well, we spoke to your family, and there does not appear to be—"

"Book me!" I interrupt.

"But there does not appear to be any domestic issue here," the officer insists.

"Arrest me! Shithead!" I demand.

The officer keeps his composure and merely grimaces at me.

"Look, man, I completely understand why you do not want to go back in there. But I have no charges for which to take you in." And with that, he puts his pen back in his shirt pocket. "Have a nice evening"

For a moment, I am tempted to punch him in the nose, simply for an extra charge for which to be booked.

I slowly make my way back into the house. Now it is time for the moment my grandmother dreaded. I step inside hesitantly and see my aunt Genny leaning against the table, covering her eyes with her hand. Dr. Frenz is sitting on the couch, with his handlers, still holding his side. I nod to him in apology, and he nods back, this time without the air of authority that may have launched the uncontrollable fist in the first place. I then see the decrepit old man, helpless in his wheelchair, his face immobilized by his oxygen mask. His frail body appears as though it takes all his energy to simply hold himself upright. If my aunt Josie thinks the parishioners at the Presbyterian church look helpless and old, they epitomize health and vitality, compared to the poor figure in this wheelchair. This is Karl Frenz.

⸻ ((◉)) ⸻

Loire Valley, France, 1942

Anso looked to see Corporal Karl Frenz pointing his rifle at Strobel, ignoring the fact that the other two soldiers were ready to shoot him.

The young corporal who helped her hide little Thomas was now pointing a weapon at Strobel. The young corporal who ordered her father to construct a frame of Adolph Hitler and the same young corporal whose face she spit in was now saving her family once more.

"Get out! All of you!" young Corporal Frenz demanded. "I will shoot!" he warned.

"Corporal, have you lost your mind? My men will shoot."

"Let them! You can explain it to Major Engel! We both know that if you have his driver executed, you had better be able to produce the young man in question! Because if you cannot!" the corporal did not have to finish. Strobel knew theoretically, the corporal was right.

Frenz cocked his weapon, and Strobel held up his hand to his soldiers, as if to wave them off.

"Worry not, young corporal! We will talk later!" Strobel said as the three of them walked out of the apartment. "Just remember, Corporal, you won't belong to Major Engel forever. Your time will come, and I won't forget this."

Frenz kept his gaze affixed on Strobel as he exited the door and did not reaffix his gaze until Strobel had closed the door behind him, casting one last glance at the corporal. Mademoiselle Chevalier ran to the corporal and buried her head in his shoulders as she cried.

"Merci Beaucoup Monsieur! Thank you for helping us!"

"Why are you helping us?" Monsieur Chevalier demanded, frustrated. "And is this going to come back on us."

"The answer to both of those questions, I don't know!" was Frenz's only answer.

Monsieur Chevallier continued to fret.

"Strobel is going to make us pay!" he insisted.

"No, he will not. I will not let him. I will get Engel on his ass if I must."

"And if that does not work?"

"I have other plans!" Frenz responded cooly.

"What's going to happen to you?" Monsieur Chevalier asked Frenz

"Don't you worry, sir! I am going to kill Strobel!" Frenz promised the family.

Redemption is the act of righting one's wrong, the making and offering of reparations for past indiscretions. Frenz had more than redeemed his associations with Engel's troops and more than redeemed his confronting Anso in the tabac. Frenz was redeemed.

Five

MORBID IRONY

"I don't understand!" Aunt Genny sob. "I don't understand! How could you do this to dad?"

"Honeypot! This was before your father," my grandmother says, nearly unapologetically.

"It was immediately before your father! I actually knew him," the old man, Frenz, replies in a crackling voice.

"Nobody is talking to you!" my aunt commands, now regaining her solid, tough composure, for which I have always known her.

While Aunt Josie holds barely any resemblance to her namesake, Josephine, Aunt Genevieve is a pinpoint-accurate clone of her mother's once best friend. I never knew nor bothered to ask if any of my aunts and uncles or cousins had heard the intimate details of the stories of my grandmother's past.

"Well, I barely considered him my father, regardless!" my father says under his breath.

"Well, naturally," I think to myself, "because he was not."

The room falls silent at the sting of a truth I have known for too long. Time never can drown out the truth; like a message in a bottle, it surfaces eventually. I know I am my grandmother's favorite, but never knew why. I was always the one in trouble. The oldest of all the cousins, and the first son of the one who was the firecracker among his siblings, my only remaining speculation is that I so adopted and embraced the French culture, to which the remainder of her children and grandchildren appear apathetic.

I visited her many times throughout my time in college and in the army. Never had I too many friends, nor did I care. I would have rather visited my grandmother and listened to her stories about her friend Genevieve, her farm, and all the animals she had. The first time I heard her tell me about Corporal Karl Frenz and who he was to me, I was nearly shell-shocked. I had lived over twenty years believing I was somebody I was not. My own father lived over fifty years likewise. After some beers, some time, and some rationalizing, I could understand perfectly how somebody could fall for anybody in her circumstances and could more than understand why she would never want anybody to know the truth of that matter. Now the truth is resurfacing.

"So, does this make you happy?" Uncle Keys's wife asks indiscriminately and with some annoyance. "I mean, what in the hell is your purpose coming here?"

Karl Frenz looks up at her pathetically. "I am dying, and wanted to see her one last time before I go," he says, gesturing toward my grandmother.

"How sweet," she hisses, "must be nice, that you have that chance. Your victims, some of whom were little children when you killed them in those concentration camp infernos, did not get that courtesy." Uncle Keys's wife, Roselynn, is as fiery as she is beautiful. My uncle met her when she was a visiting student from Israel. She has long, black hair and olive skin. Her mother was a child survivor from the Dachau death camp. So ravaged from malnourishment was her devastated little body that it was determined by Allied Force doctors that she would never again walk, and certainly never birth children. However, she not only developed her legs but became an accomplished athlete and gave birth to her daughter, twenty years after her rescue, making Roselynn Aunt Josie's age. She was even selected to compete in track in the Olympics at one point, in her thirties, but the deficiencies she suffered as a child in the death camp were just enough to wreck her training endurance required for such a feat. As defeated as her mother felt, she did not realize how it saved her life. The woman who beat her and took her place on the Israeli track team was shot dead in Munich, in 1973, when a Palestinian movement captured and killed Israeli athletes, on Roselynn's ninth birthday.

"I am going to bed!" Roselynn declares, storming out frustrated. At this point, it is only me, Aunt Josie, and my grandmother who remain with the great professor, Dr. Karl Frenz Jr, and his near-invalid father.

I have to admit that I thoroughly enjoy the irony of it. Dr. Karl Frenz Jr., or the professor, as the world knows him, is in my grandmother's living room. Dr. Frenz is the intellectual authority on every socioeconomic or sociopolitical event in the world. Every intellectually minded snob who fancies themselves a scholar worships the professor. The professor has been interviewed by Dan Rather and Anderson Cooper and is consulted on the twenty-four-hour news network to comment on anything from Iraq, Afghanistan, Zimbabwe, China, and the rest of the world. I would have always imagined that Aunt Genny and Uncle Keys would love even the smallest chance to talk with the great Dr. Frenz. Now here he is, and shamefully escorting a living, disabled stain on our ennobled family.

"Well, this has been a rough night!" my grandmother declares justifiably. She comes over and kisses me on the cheek, and then Josie. She then approaches Karl Frenz.

"You will stop by tomorrow?"

The frail old man simply shakes his head as he feebly grabs my grandmother's hand, refusing to let go, but only looking at her with a pleading, sorrowful look. Then his son steps in.

"We will stop by briefly, and then we will be on the road. I have to be back in Atlanta." For the first time in many years, everyone in the room ignores the great professor.

So here we are. The television host, my aunt Josie, a grandfather I only knew about but a few years ago, and me.

"Well, I suppose the almighty Professor Frenz is driving, so let's all have some drinks!" I say, rubbing my hands together. As my alcoholism spiraled out of control, never did there exist either a bad time or a bad reason to serve up a drink, but late in the evening, within the warm sanctity of my grandmother's farm, is an ideal time.

"Jesus Christ! Look at him!" Dr. Frenz scold me. "What in the hell is the matter with you! The last thing he needs—"

"Oh, shut up!" the old man cuts him off as he removes his oxygen mask. "I'll take a scotch, drop of water, and one ice cube. That means, less than two!" He grins.

I am only too happy to oblige. Josie, Karl, and I happily sip our drinks, and then our second ones. At some point, we move out to the porch that spans the perimeter of the house, and to the disapproving chagrin of Dr. Frenz, marijuana is furnished. Aunt Josie is shameless enough that she can be the only one indulging without so much as a care if anyone else was partaking, which I find is rare for pot enthusiasts, who always insist you join in. While I have never been a fan of pot, she has a companion in Old Man Karl, who gladly indulges as Dr. Frenz has a hopeless look on his face.

Before long, scotch and waters become the bottle on the table, accompanied by some smoke, and we even talk the professor into indulging into a drink and a puff.

"I wanted to see Anso one last time!" Frenz insists.

"Why did you wait so long? I mean, certainly you knew that she married an American soldier, but..." Being the only one who knows the whole story, I cannot finish the question.

"You see the uproar that I have caused. Can you imagine the uproar had I reached out while your grandfather was still alive? Look, I refrained out of respect!" the old man declares unapologetically.

"Well, it's really the idea that you had the balls to come to the house that our father built for his family after defeating you people. That is what asses everyone up!" Josie explains, clearly lit by now.

Well, even a lit Aunt Josie has a point.

Irony. Irony is the incongruity between what would have been expected and what may have actually occurred. Morbid irony, however, is the fantastical expectation of the most dreadful, not realizing that this will be the actual result.

Loire Valley, 1944

Captain Victor Carlson plastered himself to the cold French soil, camouflaging himself in the frigid pitch dark that the blacked-out night offered as he watched the red lights of German aircraft fly above him.

"Idiots! Do they not realize how easy they are to spot here?" he whispered to himself, mentally cursing his soldiers' disregard of light discipline. *Light discipline,* defined in the manual, is the concealment from the observation of the enemy in the air and on the ground of revealing luminous signs of troops. It is one of the first things that an infantryman learns. Nevertheless, here were his soldiers sucking down cigarettes with German aircraft just above them. From over fifty yards behind, he could look back and see the expanding red lights of the cigarette cherries each time one of them inhaled. Wonderful. He knew the crew on those aircraft only had to look down and see scattered red cigarette cherries lighting up the field and the flickering of matches lighting them and need only drop one bomb to wipe out most if not his entire company. He scrambled on his belly up the field and grabbed his executive officer, Lorinzini.

"Damnnit! There must be seven or eight people smoking! We have German aircraft hovering right over us! Crawl back there and get the first sergeant on this!"

"Captain! You want me to crawl over a hundred yards back? We are almost on point at the objective!"

Lorinzini was a tall, dark, young guy known throughout the battalion for his common sense. Captain Carlson thought for a moment. He was right. They were a couple of hours before sunrise, and then the cigarettes would not be so dangerous. Also, they were just a few clicks, or kilometers, from their objective.

Vic was the youngest child of seven children, many of whom were close to fifteen years his senior. His father was a renowned Latin and Greek scholar who had also served as education super-intendent for the state of Florida. As a child, young Vic was a stut-terer, which in the 1920s was tantamount to retardation, and was also naturally left-handed, which rendered him even more of a mis-fit. I had heard many stories of his youth spent with his father tying his left arm to his body in order to compel utilization of the right appendage, his right arm.

If such humiliation were not painful enough, a very young Victor grew up in the shadow of his older, much savvier brothers, James and Rubin. By the time Vic was ten years old, Rubin was captain of the 1929 Florida Gators. Rubin's finale was facing off against the Tennessee Vols, where he faced the great Bobby Dodd, who would later coach Georgia Tech in Atlanta.

Victor endured the loneliness and humiliation and did the best he could, existing in the shadows of his accomplished brothers, doing his best to forge his own legacy. He finished law school and eventually joined the FBI, in 1941. By his second year, Vic was tasked with chasing down deserters, or draft dodgers. His work was bor-ing as he chased down dead-end leads of family members, forged and welded by their past decade hardship of the Depression, who refused to give up their family. So sorry did Vic feel for these fami-lies, already ravished by the Depression, and so little did he think of those whom he was chasing, that he decided to hang up his fed-eral badge and enlist in the United States Army as an infantryman. He finished his basic training at Fort Benning, was selected and completed Officer Candidate School, and would then join a new and innovative program, where he would train to jump off of two-hundred-foot towers, just across from where he attended Officer Candidate School. He would become a new type of soldier that the US was fielding, who would be parachuted into zone, airborne.

It had been barely sixteen weeks since the Allies, by storming Normandy Beach, first and finally penetrated the Nazi stronghold in France. Yet to him, it seemed like over a year he had been marching deeper into France, stabbing more inroads into what was tightly held Nazi territory since 1940.

It had only been months since his plane was blown out of the sky during the invasion of Normandy, France. Vic only remembered lining up along the inside of the plane, as the red light flashed, and a gust of frigid air burst through the opening hatch with the harsh buzzing and screams of the jump sergeants ordering the troops out of the hatch. Carlson only remembered taking his one last step off the black metal of the plane and his next into the frigid blackness of the northern French night. After that he sensed an explosive burst of light, followed by a booming sound that deafened him, and his back, from neck to his heel, felt as though on fire, just as his parachute broke from the static line, thus forcing open his chute as he helplessly dangled over the black landscape of northern rural France. Lucky for him that a static line upon which his chute was fixed was by design to open the chute by itself. For after the explosion, Carlson was momentarily unconscious and would have never pulled the chute himself.

Seconds later, he awoke floating helplessly in midair, unaware of where he was. When he awoke, he had no idea that most of his unit had been wiped out by German surface-to-air artillery that had managed to blow his unit's plane out of the sky. By the time he forcefully landed, nearly blowing out his legs, as a result of his failing to keep his knees together due to his unconsciousness, he was nearly forty kilometers off course. He had no idea that he was miles within the rural territory of northern France. He was still groggy from the explosion, still had no idea where he was, and had the least bit of appreciation for the fact that he was in Nazi territory.

Vic was one of hundreds of Allied soldiers who had landed behind the treacherous Nazi lines. The worst day of Supreme Allied Commander General Eisenhower's life was having to inform Chief of Staff of the Army (who at that time was the equivalent of the chairman of the joint chiefs of staff) General George C. Marshall, that enough soldiers to make up a whole division of troops were scattered behind German lines, unaccounted for.

Luckily, Vic was found by a squad from the 101st Airborne Division, part of a battalion that had begun patrolling to round up fleeing smaller German units. The rural areas surrounding the French northern coasts became instant no-man's-lands. Smaller German units would flee inland in an effort to link up with their higher headquarters. In the meantime, they would round up US soldiers blown off course from the invasion and take them prisoner. In some instances, those smaller German units would be apprehended by companies of US infantry penetrating south and westward. This cat-and-mouse game continued for weeks, following the invasion.

Once Vic was recovered and brought safely back to the coast, he was informed of the loss of his unit. Vic was immediately promoted to captain and given a company in a new unit that had lost four junior officers during the invasion. His new unit marched westward to St Lo, then continued southward, taking city by city. Some cities did not go so easily, and Carlson's company lost many men. The Germans desperately clung to northern France, understanding that an Allied grip on northern France meant an easy march into Berlin. Nevertheless, Vic's unit, along with many others, took city by city and marched on eastward and eventually made their way south. The farther the Allies progressed, the easier it was, as Germans began to flee, seeing the obvious.

Now it was late November of 1944, and Carlson's next objective was a small town situated less than a hundred yards in front of him. This was the first mission where he had to airborne drop since the Normandy invasion. The town his company was taking was so far south in the Loire Valley as to render it impractical to march down there and would have taken too much time. Carlson's company was to parachute approximately twenty miles north of the city so that the aircraft could avoid detection. They would then march down to the city, take the city from what British intel had reported was a weakened Wehrmacht sturm stubbornly holding the city. Carlson's company was to defeat the German unit and prepare the city for the rest of his battalion to arrive in and establish a holding, further securing Allied presence in central France, from which Allied units could continue to chase and capture fleeing German units.

The company dropped into central France in the middle of the night. The minute his ankles hit the turf, his knees felt as though they would bust out. His first sergeant noticed that he was not yet up and packing his chute, and discreetly came to his rescue and helped him up.

They spent the evening marching eight miles south and set up a perimeter to rest at the time the sun arose over a deceptively peaceful and tranquil French countryside. Carlson looked away from the blinding morning sun that had crept up behind a desolate Atlantic coast hundreds of miles away. He looked west at the shadows the sun had cast upon the silent green pastures, contrasting the untouched grass, moistened by the morning summer dew.

"I wonder what this place looked like before the Germans took over?" he whispered to his first sergeant.

"Probably no different," the first sergeant replied, barely looking over but rousing his troops for an afternoon march that would take them into the early evening.

Carlson wanted to allow his soldiers to talk among themselves as they were still miles from the German held city. However, his first sergeant insisted the soldiers started to exercise noise discipline immediately.

"Sir, if they do not start noise discipline until we are close to the objective, then it will never start. If we start enforcing silence now, then by the time we get on objective, it will start!"

"Good point!" Carlson agreed. Every good junior officer knew to listen to their top enlisted sergeant. Carlson learned this lesson as a platoon leader when his unit was back stateside, getting ready to ship to Britain. During that time, Carlson's platoon sergeant whipped his troops into shape and made the impossible happen. Every officer understood that while they gave the orders, it was their higher sergeants, or noncommissioned officers, who made the orders happen.

"Not to mention, this close out, the Wehrmacht could have LP/ Ops out here!"

Carlson only nodded his head as he collected his gear. It was doubtful that the Germans would have LP/Ops, or lookout post, observational posts. From what Carlson read in the operations order, this sturm was on their last leg, with some Germans having already deserted. It was only at the stubbornness of the commander that they still occupied the city and had not fled as other units had done.

The company continued to march south late into the afternoon and had made thirteen miles, shouldering heavy gear and weaponry, before the first sergeant silently raised his fist and silently through field hand signals ordered his troops to take a knee and prepare a hasty perimeter where they would rest before resuming their remaining two miles at dusk. The soldiers formed a perimeter, and two or three posted themselves guard. For the next four hours, each soldier would take turns posting guard, while everyone else changed their socks and readjusted their gear. Once darkness fell upon the countryside, and the air was pitch-black, Carlson's company would reinitiate their march. Now was the time, they had to execute every move perfectly. They were well within sound and sight of any German guard that could have been posted, hence why they waited an hour into dark night to recommence their march toward the city. Hand signals would not work now, as it was so dark that the soldiers could barely see in front of them. Now communications were done through tapping the man behind. Once they had marched a short but excruciatingly slow mile and a half, Captain Carlson slapped his first sergeant, who began a domino effect where each soldier would slowly crouch down to their knees and then to their bellies. The last leg of the approach would be low-crawled. They would halt a tenth of a kilometer short of the guarded gate, wait until just before dawn to initiate their surprise assault. Carlson needed this city under complete control before the rest of his battalion would arrive in two days.

Carlson and his company lay low in the barren fields, taking cover behind anything they could find, while observing the unsuspecting, complacent Wehrmacht soldiers who guarded the chain-length fence. He motioned for Lorinzini to move his platoon up to the ridge as his first squad situated their machine gunner and moved to flank the right side of the fence's gate, where the German was guarding. Zini's platoon's second squad slowly maneuvered to flank the left side of the gate entrance. Carlson silently nodded at Zini, and Zini gave a signal upon which both squads' machine gun fired a series of rounds that hit just inches from the German's boots, coming simultaneously from both directions. The soldier immediately took cover, too overwhelmed to start returning fire. The first squad immediately moved up on the soldier, their weapons fixed upon the surprised German solder. He awkwardly put up his hands, realizing he was seriously outgunned. Zini silently got up and quickly moved to his first squad, bringing one soldier with him but still maintaining a half-composed posture of concealment that only consisted of him flexing his shoulders and ducking his head.

Zinni slightly tapped the soldier with his backhand.

"Go, Pierson!" he said in his thick New York accent, and Pierson began growling German demands.

"Give up your weapons and open the gate silently!" Pierson demanded as he strained a whisper loud enough to command, but also trying to conceal.

Carlson watched attentively as Zini's platoon moved into position within the city proper. Upon satisfaction that Zini's platoon was in place and their snipers were set, Carlson carefully signaled the rest of his company, the other platoons creeping up along the perimeter of the small city to support their main effort, Zini's platoon. Closing in on the city and blending with the buildings, the supporting elements tossed some grenades toward the roving Germans they spotted to startle them. Once the grenades went off, the second and third platoon laid down a constant suppressing fire, hitting as many Germans as they could see and hitting them as many times as they could. Meanwhile, Zini's platoon continued to creep up the main street of the city in two columns, each one on each side of the street, flush with the buildings that housed the startled French, and even some Germans that knew the Americans had arrived. Carlson came up behind Zini's platoon up the main street to take the hotel de ville.

Carlson's mission to take the city lasted most of the day, and his company sustained casualties, mostly from the platoons acting as support elements, but a few from Zini's platoon were hit in the head by snipers Engel had placed on the roof of the cathedral. Carlson knew that the German army that was once so feared and powerful were now demoralized and scared as the past six months made them well aware of their mortality as a fighting force. Carlson was surprised that Major Engel was even holding out here, as most of the cities through which his company marched were already abandoned by fleeing German units. Although Hitler had ordered his Wehrmacht to hold down the French cities in effort to hold off Allies and maintaining most of France as he could, many Germans, nevertheless, fled and in some cases begged the Americans to take them prisoner. However, this unit fought viciously to the last and did not intend to give up the city. After close to two thirds of the Wehrmacht were shot, and once Zini's platoon had the hotel de ville surrounded, with the other two platoons in tactical control of the remainder of the city, Engel had but little choice.

Zini's first two squads lined up and formed a *V* in front of the hotel de ville, taking cover where they could, be it a café or lamppost, aiming their rifles. Carlson stood at the bottom of the steps holding his weapon and with Zini's soldier, Pierson, next to him. Carlson whispered something to Pierson, and Pierson blared out in perfect German that commanded all occupants to slowly march out of the building with their hands on their head. Major Engel first emerged, and two soldiers rushed up on him to check him. Once they were satisfied that he was clear, they shoved him down the stairs, were he stood face-to-face with Captain Carlson.

"I am Captain Vic Carlson, Company C Commander of 5th Battalion, 3rd Brigade, of 513th Airborne Division."

"I am Major Engel." He paused. "No salute, Captain? You do not salute superior officers? What a bad example to set for your men, who will surely pattern this disgraceful behavior." Carlson was amazed at how calm and collected he was, as the rest of his soldiers were clearly frightened and agitated. Another one of Carlson's soldiers was aggressively patting down a German corporal for con-cealed weapons, as the German soldier kept his hands plastered to his head.

"Sir! He speaks English and French!" the soldier declared.

"Good! Bring him here!" Carlson commanded.

"What is your name?" Carlson asked the soldier.

"Corporal Frenz," he replied.

"You are going to stay with me!" Carlson commanded.

"Say, 'Yes sir,' dipshit!" the soldier spat as he slapped Frenz across the back of his head. Carlson put up his hand as to signal enough.

Carlson looked up to see another German officer being shuffled down the stairs. Carlson remembered the venomous look in his black eyes.

"Sir, this guy is...Strobel," a soldier with a Southern accent said.

"Okay, get Lieutenant Dillingham," Carlson ordered. He spun back around toward Engel, who was still intently staring him in the eye. Carlson feebly saluted him, and Engel executed a sharp salute in return.

"Now get on your knees, sir, and keep your hands by your side," he ordered Engel and pointed at his soldiers to do likewise with Strobel and the others found in the hotel de ville.

Just then, a ragged-looking soldier ran up to Carlson.

"Sir?"

"Dillingham! What is your final count?" Carlson asked.

The bigger lieutenant, a lumberjack from Oregon who looked so much older than Captain Carlson, slowly removed his helmet, where his shaggy hair fell out.

"Captain, two of my guys are down. Germans hiding in some of the shops, hit 'em, and I got a medic on one guy hit in the stomach."

"Is he gonna make it?" Carlson drilled him.

"Not sure, Captain. Medic is havin' trouble stopping the bleed-ing, and blood is coming out of his mouth."

Carlson grimaced at the diagnosis that in itself was obvious without mention.

"Okay. Dillingham, listen to me. I need you to go to the police station for the city, free the French citizens who are currently in there. Take Pierson with you and have him inform the gendarmerie there that the city is secured. We are expecting the battalion command, staff, and supporting elements to arrive within the next twenty-four to forty-eight hours and that you are going to be temporary provost, only until higher arrives. Also, inform those gendarmeries that we will need as much room as possible for the remaining Germans."

Just then, Carlson felt a wave of discontentment. He heard shocked sighs and an overall energy of disapproval overtook him.

"Sir, they did not surrender. They killed some of our men!" Carlson's first sergeant reminded him.

"We take them prisoner, we cannot execute them," Carlson whispered to his senior NCO.

"Sir, not only are the townspeople watching you but so are the soldiers. They just lost some of their brothers not only with whom they marched halfway through this country but some of these soldiers have not been separated since their initial basic training!" the aggravated first sergeant declared through gritted teeth.

Carlson did not have to turn around to face his first sergeant. He could feel the scrutinous stare of his NCO, and he agreed with him but also knew what the new laws were concerning German captives. He turned around to face the first sergeant. First Sergeant Lightfoot was much older than Carlson. His story was quite common, having run away from home at age fifteen and concealing his real age to sign up with the army in 1918, as the US was closing the First World War. At the conclusion of the war, Lightfoot had no inclination to leave the army, knowing there was no life for him on the desolate Oklahoma reservation from where he grew up. Now, nearly twenty-six years later, he had survived every major battle of the European theater, starting under Patton's third corps in Algeria, to Sicily, in the Allies' failed attempt at penetrating the Nazi held European continent through the "underbelly," to a year later having been part of the successful breach in Normandy. Behind the first sergeant's back, his soldiers called him the Owl, for his thin, bony but haggard face, offset by his big, black, harrowing eyes, when he stared down his company.

"I don't know." Carlson nearly begged timidly, hoping his company leadership would accept his plea.

"Sir, we should at least kill the leadership. Just the officers," Zini added, having overheard the conversation. "That way, we have prisoners to show for when the colonel arrives tomorrow, and we only snipe those who insisted on fighting and costing us lives! You know, those that gave the orders to fight."

Carlson sighed, then drew a deep breath. He looked around the city. Most of the French cities he had seen up north were mere shells of what were once great historical monuments of a thousand years of Western civilization. Charred skeletons were what remained of these great architectural feats of the Middle Ages. Yet this city was untouched by the land-shattering Allied shelling and thus an intact remainder of the pleasant lifestyle enjoyed by the French before the iron steel of the German war machine trampled its existence. He looked around the street and saw timid French citizens peeking out of their shops, some courageously emerging to see Engel and Strobel get their due. The past two years had been especially traumatic as Germans began to lose ground; life for the occupied citizens became worse.

"Wonderful!" Zini exclaimed as though the decision had been made in Captain Carlson's long pause. "We will start with him!" And he pointed at a frightened looking German lieutenant. Lieutenant Pete Lorinzini, a Brooklyn native, was Carlson's executive officer. After the lieutenant who led the first platoon was killed by a German sniper in the Bretagne region, Lorinzini, always called "Zini," now served as the XO as well as the first platoon leader, as Carlson waited months for a replacement. While never getting a new LT was aggravating, Carlson secretly thanked God. Zini was an excellent leader. He was tall, dark, lanky but built, and never afraid to make a decision. Zini was the polar opposite of Carlson. Carlson descended from a family of Southern gentlemen who valued manners, quiet demeanor, tradition, and rules. Zini was a second generation of Italian immigrants. He grew up fighting on the immigrant-flooded New York streets. He was loud and abrasive, and to him, tradition and rules were but impediments to his ultimate goals, be they sex with a girl in the village or killing the enemy. Once again, Zini had no problem making decisions for his captain, whose adherence to rules sometimes rendered him frozen and indecisive.

"What's your name shithead!" Zini demanded from the frightened German kid.

"Wie lautet dein name?" the young German soldier next to Carlson had shouted out.

"Benzinger," the young officer said in barely a muffled whisper.

Zini turned his attention toward the young German translator.

"And who the hell are you?" he commanded.

"Corporal Frenz," the soldier said, still standing next to Carlson with his hands on his head.

"Okay get over there with the other captive soldiers."

"No!" commanded Carlson, as he signaled toward Frenz. "He stays with us for the time being. We may need him. Pierson speaks some German, but this guy seems fluent in English. We hold onto him at least until higher rolls through here."

Zini turned his attention back to Benzinger and motioned for him to get up on the platform in front of the church.

More citizens emerged from their shops as they watched a visibly frightened Benzinger backed up onto the same stage where Major Engel first addressed them, in what seemed like an eternity passed. Carlson turned his back and faced the growing crowd as he placed his hands on his hips, unable to look into young Benzinger's helpless, now puppy-dog-like eyes.

Monsieur Chevalier felt a tinge of guilt as he tried to bury the welled-up pleasure he experienced seeing Benzinger standing on the stage, so shaken and frightened. Chevalier actually began to pity Benzinger. He imagined that Benzinger was a good kid, who at an early age attended one of Germany's military academies and inundated with their militaristic ideals from a young, impressionable age. During the years the French suffered under Engel's occupation, Benzinger seemed the most yearning for professionalism and reason.

If Carlson could not stand to look at Benzinger, Zini had no problem. The shot rang out, and Carlson turned around just in time to see the pistol jerk Zini's arm upward. Carlson turned completely around to see a lifeless, slumped Benzinger sliding against the wall, leaving behind a trail of blood on that old stone wall, his now lifeless eyes wide and bulging out. Out of his peripheral, Carlson could see Zini motion for the next. The black haired German captain did not go as quietly. Strobel begged and pleaded for his life. Standing him up on the stage was impossible. After two failed attempts where Strobel was literally clinging to one of Zini's sergeants, Zini finally ordered two troops to hold each side. This time Carlson watched on as tears streamed down Strobel's face, and he closed his eyes, just as Zini fired his pistol into Strobel's exploding chest. Each of the other three German captains and dozens of junior officers took their fatal turn on the stage, under Zini's pistol. They all reacted in between Benzinger's fear and Strobel's all-out pathetic pleading. One lieutenant grabbed on to Zini's sleeve and pulled out a letter he had penned to his parents in living in Darmstadt. Zini slapped the letter away and ordered him on the stage. Victor Carlson kneeled down and picked up the letter and placed it in his pocket, just as the gunshot ended the life of its author.

Major Engel remained on his knees as he watched every subordinate officer of his sturm executed, every one of his enlisted troops carted away, and his personal secretary and driver confiscated by Carlson.

"Okay, your turn!" Zini ordered to Engel. "On your feet!" He then turned to Carlson and handed him the sidearm. "Sir, the soldiers need to see you do one of these!"

"Captain!" Engel called out. "I order you to give me delay my execution until tomorrow!"

Carlson was amazed at this man's audacity.

"Who the hell do you think you are, giving orders to the captain!" Zini screamed.

"I am a major in my army."

"You are a piece of shit, in a losing shattered Army!" Zini shouted as he spit in Engel's face.

A stream of saliva dripped down Engel's face.

"Captain! If you fail to discipline your soldiers and allow them to show such gross disrespect to superior officers, enemy or friendly, then you they will lose respect for all military discipline and decorum. When your prisoners of war, who are officers, are captured by German forces, we require our enlisted address them as such. Wartime and combat should offer you no luxuries and certainly should offer you no excuse to drop your military courtesies. Discipline is what holds a unit together in cohesion. Its failure will crumble your structure, and thus your effort."

Carlson had to admit he was impressed by Engel's adherence to military tradition, even in the face of impending death.

"Major, sir!" Carlson interjected. "You are a captured soldier. You do not give me orders. If you should so request more time, I will consider it. But make no mistake! The decision will be mine, and mine alone, even if made at the advice of my junior officer and top NCO! Being so engrained in military discipline, as you are, clearly you understand my position! Go ahead and take him away. He gets one night in jail." And Carlson turned away.

"You come with me," he ordered Frenz.

Carlson took Frenz and headed up to the mayor's office.

"Well, you can start by cleaning out this office!" Carlson ordered Frenz.

Just then, Carlson heard a knock at the door, and Zini walked in the door.

"Sir, Major Engel wants"—he then cleared his throat—"wants his dress uniform and wishes to polish his brass, for tomorrow morning."

"Okay, well, it is a good thing you caught me now." Carlson replied, "I was about to clean this all out in whole swoop! You!" He directed his orders at Frenz. "Get these uniforms down to the jail. Zini, get one of your guys to escort him there and back. I want someone on him at all times."

That night, Carlson slept in the office that once belonged to Mayor Bourgeois, then to Engel, and now it was Carlson who was preparing it to be a workstation for the arrival of his battalion commander in the next two days.

The morning arrived too quickly, and Carlson thought his head had hit the floor but only minutes prior. Frenz was making coffee and arranging Carlson's affairs. Carlson made his way to the police station to visit with Lieutenant Dillingham, his temporary provost marshal, until the remainder of the unit arrived.

"We should leave him here, until higher arrives," Carlson thought out loud to his second platoon leader.

"Sir, he is ready to go, though. I mean he was up all night, shining his brass, going through his notes. I even saw him pray," Dillingham said with a confused look on his face.

Carlson walked down to the jail where the same Germans who once proudly waltzed carefree about the city were now locked down in a somber, crowded chamber. In a solitary cell, Major Engel was standing up, dressed down in his formal wear, complete with his swastika band, and his hands clasped behind his back, as though he were still running the city in his ruthless but professional manner. Carlson thought of the stories his father told him, about polishing General Lee's brass, and how immaculately he presented himself just prior to surrendering to a slovenly looking Grant known for being obnoxiously drunk.

Carlson could not turn back now, even though he wanted so bad to leave him in jail. Overnight, the word escaped that Major Engel was going to be shot, and a crowd was already gathering first thing in the morning. Yet, Carlson paid them no mind. He was doing this for his men. He knew it was wrong and was dragged nearly kicking and screaming to shoot Engel but knew his men needed to see him shot. Carlson wanted so badly to explain that shooting somebody would not bring back Carter, Dooley, Crandle, McAllister, and the others who died yesterday. Nevertheless, the men counted on him. He understood the dire importance of maintaining their trust and respect, even though in less than two months it would not matter. Every one of his men would no longer be alive.

"Sir, he left a letter for you," Dillingham produced the letter to Carlson, looking puzzled.

Equally a puzzled, Carlson looked at Dillingham before opening the folded paper.

I write to you in humble apology for the cowardly behavior of my officers yesterday afternoon and appeal to your good senses as an officer yourself to assert the blame on my failure of leadership and refrain from indicting them personally for their less than stoic behavior.

Incredible, Carlson thought. This guy was accountable for the deaths and exterminations of a good fraction of this small city in the four years he had contained it within his iron grip. He was part of a force that would forever be synonymous with systematic evil. Even the most severe and vile of his army's depraved evils were yet to even be uncovered as they were still months from liberating the concentration camps. Yet Engel's biggest regret prior to being marched off to his death was his junior officers' less-than-enthusiastic attitude toward being publicly shot.

For the first time since he was first parachuted into France back in June, Carlson realized exactly what he was dealing with. He now understood how dedicated this enemy was and the resolve that burned within them. Engel looked to be in his early forties, meaning, he could have fought in the First World War as a teenager, just like his first sergeant, Lightfoot. But unlike Lightfoot, he appeared much younger and vibrant. Engel, like his fuehrer, had experienced the worldly humiliation and scorn that preceded the Treaty of Versailles. And like his fuehrer, he suffered through the ghastly depression that followed their harsh penalty of the Treaty of Versailles that hit the country with a $9 billion reparation bill. Engel was most likely one of the millions of young men in their twenties with no hope of a future in a depression that made America's Depression look prosperous. He was one of many whose family's life savings could now not so much as purchase a cup of coffee. It was not difficult to believe that by his early thirties, a void hopeless future, divested of any hope, now started to spring up in economic powerhouse under the new chancellor. Before he knew it, Engel was now well on his feet and a commissioned officer under one of the most powerful armies since Genghis Khan's Mongols or Julius Caesar's Rome, both of whom overran half the world. Never would Engel, not even in front of Carlson's pistol, ever abandon his most revered and idolized fuehrer.

Carlson shuddered, and now was energized with fear but for the first time in his life, inspired anger.

"First Sergeant! Get him up to the square!" he commanded, and the first sergeant happily obliged. He grabbed Engel by the arm and assisted his NCO to forcefully escort Engel up to the square. The rapidly growing crowd, amassing to see justice finally served, was overwhelming, but Carlson barely noticed. He focused his aim at the top of Engel's head, but was overwhelmed by Engel's calm acceptance and even Engel's polite nod of approval, as though they were business associates. In Engel's mind, they were. They were both in the profession of arms, merely on opposing sides. Carlson aimed his weapon with less than a steady hand. He closed his eyes, then opened them quickly and was staring right into the solid-blue eyes of Engel. Victor had soft-blue eyes, but Engel's were slight, stern, and piercing, and they pierced right through the young captain. Victor quickly closed them and opened them again for just long enough to steady his shaky aim. He closed his eyes once more and forcefully pulled the trigger and quickly opened them to make sure he had at least hit his target in front of all these villagers. No sooner had he opened his eyes did he see Engel's head jerk back and a splattered streak of dark red blood paint the old medieval wall of the old church behind. So surreal was the moment Carlson barely noticed the cheers of the roaring crowd. Nor did he notice

Zini's platoon subsequently rushing up on the stage to prevent a small mob of French youth from tearing apart Engel's now limp body.

Carlson simply stood there, aghast and awestruck that he was capable of killing an unarmed, helpless individual. He knew he was not supposed to kill surrendered captives. However, would a guy like Engel ever really surrender?

"Hey, Captain, we could use some assistance up here!" Vic was immediately interrupted as Zini screamed as he was holding back a young French kid who had taken out a knife and was ready to unzip Engel's urine-stinking trousers. Carlson shook out of his temporarily trance and shouted at the first sergeant to get more troops from the third platoon to help contain the near riot about to erupt. While Zini was wrestling off the kid and disarming him, the rest of the soldiers had been able to cordon off the body and control the cheering, surrounding citizens. Carlson looked back and saw a young girl with dark hair who had managed to lug a heavy cinder block up the three steps and was hoisting it over Engel's paralyzed face. He snuck up behind her, and grabbed the brick, slowly guiding it down and out of her hand. Their gaze met, and he was momentarily captivated by her dark, pretty but melancholy eyes.

Perhaps he was too captivated. He was hypnotized just long enough for her to cough up and spit a mouth full of saliva in his face and kick Carlson in the groin. Soldiers immediately swarmed a young Anso, just before their groaning captain could wave them away with one hand, and painfully holding his crotch with another.

"Take three guys and get rid of these bodies now!" he ordered Zini.

He had completed his part. His men were content. They knew they could trust him to circumvent the sometimes-pithy rules for their sake and well-being. The local citizens were ecstatic. Carlson's shooting was not simply avenging all that they had lost. It was an act that truly symbolized their freedom, their return to life as they knew it.

"Sir!" A soldier came up and reported to Carlson. "Higher called! The battalion is delayed two days for vehicle maintenance!"

"Vehicle maintenance? We marched down all the way on foot!" Carlson muttered under this breath.

Annoyed at first, Carlson realized the extra couple of days gave his men a much-deserved rest. They could take their time and leisurely go about their duties of preparing the city for the arrival of the rest of the battalion.

This city was important because it was the furthest southern point of Nazi-governed France. Any farther south was Vichy governed until 1945 and vacated after the Americans took most of northern France. It was one of the last of the holdout cities in central France, and with Carlson's taking, France was now completely free of German occupation. The bullet that Carlson had fired into the skull of Engel was the key that opened the door of France's long, cold, four-year sentence, and the US, along with the rest of Allies, intended to maintain a heavy presence throughout the freed country.

Now Carlson had a few days to lounge in the cafés once again resurrected and brought back to life but still lacking as a result of their crumbling business under occupation and German plunder. His men enjoyed their first hot meal in weeks and their first night in a warm hotel in months. Carlson informed the town to keep careful tabs of hotel occupancy and meals and beverages consumed, for when the staff of his unit arrived and his men were paid, each business would be paid in full. Although Carlson rarely consumed alcohol, he was going to make tonight an exception and indulge in a couple glasses of wine with his hearty dinner. He had roughly forgotten his manners as he stared down at his plate, devouring his food. It had been a long time eating a hot meal in the company of anyone other than his soldiers, with whom he quickly sucked down cold C rations. So engulfed in his meal, he failed to notice the girl standing at his table. He took another sip of wine and saw the same dark-eyed girl standing there. He was going to invite her to sit down, but she had already invited herself.

"Please," he said, swallowing as he tried to motion her to sit.

"You should have allowed me to smash his face!" she said. "Nobody would care, and your precious higher-ups could not blame you. As it stands, they are going to wonder how the top of his head was blown off at such close range! They will know that all of us were disarmed!"

Carlson was impressed at how sharp she was. He thought about it for a moment.

"Well, even had I let you smash his face, the bullet wound would still be there."

"Once they saw that we mutilated the guy, they won't investigate further."

"Is tearing up the corpse of Engel going to undo what he has done? Is mutilating his corpse going to bring back your mayor that he shot?"

She rolled her eyes, sighed, and quickly got up from the table.

"You have been in Europe for maybe six months, and soon you will return to the safety of your America, as you let the equally animalistic Russians finish your job of killing these monsters. You can afford to be naive and idealistic."

"Hey," he called out after, not wanting her to leave, and sorry that he had angered her.

"Sir, another glass of wine?" the waitress asked him.

"Sure thing, Chantelle. I appreciate it." He began to appreciate the lightheaded feeling that eased the heavy burden his shoulders had carried from the beaches of Normandy, to Brest, and all the way down throughout central-northern France.

"Don't try to reason with Anso!" Chantelle warned Carlson, "Nobody has been able to do it in over twenty years, and after seeing her two best friends killed, nobody ever will, I suppose."

The next forty-eight hours were supposed to be relaxing, but Carlson could not extinguish Anso from his mind. He wanted another chance to speak with her. Perhaps this time he would not botch it. At least he could apologize to her. He learned from other townspeople that her father was a portrait artist who had a run a frame shop that had to close due to inactivity under occupation. He sat back in the desk that his battalion commander would soon occupy and thought of ways to make up to her his offense the other night.

"Corporal Frenz!" he called out. The corporal rushed in with a pair of his boots shined.

"What do you know about Anne Sophie Chevalier? You have been here for four years." The corporal just glared at him. Carlson took that to mean he was dumbfounded at the question.

"Of course! You were forbidden from comingling with civilians and probably followed your orders. I just figured, after so much time, even from outside observation, you know somebody."

Carlson finally cornered Anso and got her to agree to eat with him one evening. He had posted soldiers outside of the café where she now worked, and when she tried to slip away after her shift, they politely reminded her of her commitment.

Now that he had felt relieved about his possibilities with Anso, he could concentrate on his company preparing for the arrival of the rest of his unit. Dillingham was watching the jail as acting provost and only needed, at most, a squad of soldiers. Therefore, Carlson ordered Dillingham to have his platoon sergeant take the remainder of his platoon and alongside the newly freed townspeople start eradicating the surrounding fence. Carlson then had third platoon police up the houses on the outskirts that had been occupied by German officers. They were to discard of any German memorabilia. Personal items of the German officers were to be gathered and turned into the headquarters upon their arrival.

Carlson began to look forward to his afternoon lunches and wine with Anso.

"You know, I am glad you guys came."

"Hey! She talks!" Carlson smiled.

"Really, though! I am so glad to see those awful fences come down. I can finally travel again."

"Traveling is overrated." Carlson replied, "I never left Florida until I volunteered."

"You don't miss a right or a liberty until it has been denied. You don't miss traveling until you are imprisoned and confined," Anso said with some annoyance.

"I suppose you are correct."

"What made you volunteer to come over here? I mean, I thought they made you come or something?" Anso inquired with sincere confusion.

"Well, they draft those eligible. I was already a federal employee. I worked for the government, so I was exempt from the draft."

"So why did you volunteer?"

"Not sure, really. I guess I just figured that with so many people they had me chasing as a federal agent who had skipped the draft, I would be better useful just volunteering myself."

"Well, that is so noble," Anso mocked. "Do you regret it?" she asked pointedly. "I mean, after everything you have seen, would you do it again?"

Carlson stared at his wineglass. The rare instance of drinking and a woman's company were overwhelmingly awkward enough. Now he was faced with a question for which he knew the answer and was ashamed to say. As much as he knew how important their effort was, he was loathe to admit that if he could see into the future, and learn of the horrors he would experience, that he would not have joined those whom he was ordered to chase as an FBI agent.

"So, now that you have this newfound freedom, where do you plan on traveling?" Carlson asked, trying to change the subject.

"I want to go to Brive la Gaillard to visit my cousin Robert," she replied as Carlson looked up past his glass. "You know, they staged a rebellion and themselves overthrew and ran out the Nazis. They didn't need you guys like we did!"

Most of France south of Anso's region was self-governed so long as they comported with German authoritarian government. They were called the Vichy government. After 1942, Germany became overwhelmed as Hitler had pulled two giants, the US and the Soviet Red Army, into the war. The country and its ferocious army that so easily swallowed up the continent of Europe and most of

North Africa were now faced with a two-front battle and had awaken two giants whose own ferocious armies would force them to incur massive casualties and overwhelm and exhaust their seemingly indestructible force. The war effort was increased tenfold, and the cooperative Vichy government was deposed as the Germans occupied every French city. They left a small part of the southeastern Mediterranean coast that include Nice and Cannes for the Italians, but every other city was plundered and rationed to keep up with increased need for food and resources.

"Yes, indeed, when they heard the Allies had penetrated into France, they just staged their own resistance and chased out those creeps," Anso continued.

"Ah, you mean once the Allies landed. They knew reinforcements were on the way, and they knew that most of the Germans had either been called to the eastern front to fight the Russians or just all together fled. So, then your statement is patently untrue that the city of Brive completely staged a self-reliant resistance," Carlson countered, thus starting a back-and-forth between the two that neither of them realized would last over half a century and would prove to be an early indicator of a successful career in litigation.

"Sir!" A young sergeant reported at their table, interrupting their early dinner. "Lieutenant Lemmon wanted to report that we have completed policing the houses and the properties. They were for the most part found in good condition; we did find a few personal effects. LT Lemmon awaits further orders, sir."

"Good job, guys! I will be up there in a few minutes. You have done enough today. Lieutenant Colonel Cook will be here tomorrow in the morning." He dismissed the sergeant.

Carlson redirected his attention to Anso. "Want to be one of the first to venture outside of the fence?" Anso stared at her new friend in disbelief, then immediately and hyperactively nodded her head.

"Great! Let me get my driver!"

An hour later, Anso could peer out of her apartment and see

a procession of German vehicles, this time driven by US service members. Nevertheless, the sight of those vehicles slowly strolling up those narrow cobblestone streets still pitted her stomach. The line stopped, and the third vehicle was stopped right in front of her apartment. Captain Carlson peered, jumped out from the back seat, and moved around to open the door closest to her apartment. In her excitement to finally get to venture outside these cruel gates and return to the farm she once felt so at peace, and the farm for which she now longed, she did not notice who was driving Carlson's vehicle. Rushing out toward the jeep, Anso looked up and saw Corporal Frenz looking up at her, and their eyes met, and Frenz quickly looked down. Anso rapidly brainstormed multiple scenarios that would provide her any excuse to suddenly back out of Carlson's invitation. These were all vanquished once Carlson opened the jeep door for her. Anso suddenly remembered her long strolls up to her friend Genevieve's house. Now the drive seemed long and awkward, as Frenz was the one driving them.

"Are you ready?" The jeep had already been stopped, and Carlson had already jumped to her side to open the door, before she realized the jeep had stopped. Carlson had put out his hand, as Anso took one last glance at Frenz. She awkwardly stepped out and could somehow feel a look cast upon her.

They walked along the dirt road that Anso had daily strolled, years ago. Without Genevieve to go visit, she was happy to share this moment with the young captain. They finally strolled up in front the Benoit house. She approached the house as though it were the sight of a train wreck, cautiously and unsure. The house was empty. Monsieur Benoit had yet to return, and since his wife and daughter had been killed, he had yet to speak a word. The property was no longer the warm, inviting haven it had been prior to 1940. The German captain who had taken the house got rid of the animals and destroyed most of the plants. Anso barely recognized the place. For years, she could think of nothing else but the blissful times she spent at the house and the longing for those days to return. Now she regretted that she had ever laid eyes on it. She regretted being seen by Frenz with the American captain, and now she direly regretted coming back. How stupid was she? To think life would ever be the same after what she had been through and what had been ripped from her life.

This was once a beautiful house. This was once a blissful place, where Mademoiselle Benoit would always have the best pastries made, as she would bring Adrienne out, dressed immaculately. Mademoiselle was the best mother. It broke her heart to think her last moments were spent in the rain, on a cold, blacked-out street, insane from the fact that Adrienne's murder was karma granting her wish. It broke her heart to think her best friend's last moments were spent helplessly trying to save her mother from the depths of insanity. Goddamn those Germans! Why couldn't Carlson let her smash that jerk's face! She turned around to walk away and walked right into the captain. She buried her face in his chest; tears welled up inside her and suddenly broke like a dam. Tears gushed as she cried profusely. She gripped onto his shoulders as though she would never let go. She began to hit Vic. One second, she was enraged that the Americans were in her city, and would not let her tear apart Engel. The next second, she loved him, as he led the force that rid the city of such demons. Carlson just held her and whispered to her and comforted her best he could.

By seven the following morning, Captain Carlson was standing outside the hotel de ville, with his hands behind his back. Dawn was just breaking, but the US jeeps entering through what was only days prior an entrance gate still had their lights on. The procession of vehicles stopped just in front of the hotel de ville in the middle of the square, with French onlookers and Carlson's company standing outside in full uniform. Several soldiers jumped out followed by a soldier with a silver leaf on his helmet, who exited his jeep slower than the rest. He approached Carlson and stood in front of him, waiting impatiently.

"Sir!" Carlson seemed to inquire more than greet.

"Are we missing something, Captain?" Lieutenant Colonel White asked a confused Captain Carlson.

After a few awkward seconds, Captain Carlson figured out what his battalion commander was waiting for and came to rigid attention and executed a crisp salute.

The commander returned the salute, as now a reddened, flustered Carlson apologized, embarrassed for being called out in front of all these civilians.

"Don't worry, Captain! I understand that saluting out in the field is ill advised."

"Well, sir, it's only that saluting superior officers on the battlefield marks them for…"

"I know, I know," Lieutenant Colonel White interrupted, "it marks us to the enemy. Except there is no longer an enemy to mark us to, and this is no longer a battlefield. Your men did exceptional work, and I don't fear snipers, and pretty soon, we will be in garrison mode again. Meaning, military courtesies, customs, and discipline will once again be the norm. So, I want to see haircuts and shaving again. We are in the presence of civilians, civilians who are dependent on us, and they need to see that they can entrust their faith in us."

"Yes, sir! Well, your office is ready," Carlson replied.

"Good, let me go up and drop off some of my gear; then let's go to one of these cafés and get some breakfast."

Later in the day, Captain Carlson was giving his commander the tour of the city, going through each shop and talking with each proprietor. He spent months trekking through France in rain and chilly weather. He had lost his whole unit when his plane was blown out of the sky; only six men, including him, made it out of the plane. After losing his whole unit in an airborne drop over Normandy and being lost in northern France for the better part of two weeks, before being recovered by the 101st Airborne, he was assigned to command another airborne company. As commander of the new company, he took them city through city, clearing each one of German occupation, as they thrust farther south, driving the German hold outs from their posts. He had lost up to a third of his company. Finally, his luck was changing, and his commander choosing the café where Anso worked was but one more sign of things looking up for him.

Carlson's and Anso's eyes met, as she paced rapidly out of the café carrying beers for waiting US soldiers.

"Don't get too comfortable here, Captain," White warned him, noticing the look. "A quartermaster battalion is replacing us in a few days." He pulled papers from out of his coat pocket. "I have orders moving our regiment up to Belgium, close to the German border."

"German border?" Carlson asked in surprise.

"Roger that! We are going to be on the Belgian and German border. We are dropping into northern France. I guess Eisenhower's thinking is that since we have those dirty Krauts on the run, let's keep chasing them. I suppose the worst thing we can do is allow them to pour more reinforcements back into the country we just spent the better half of a goddamned year cleaning up."

"I don't think the Germans are going to try to retake this country. They don't seem to have the same fight they did when they held Europe. I mean they were ferocious in Italy, but now, they seem more eager to give up or run."

"I agree, Captain. I think they are way more concerned about the Russians, and I can't blame them. Those animals are twice the savages these Nazis are." Neither of them could appreciate how wrong they were, nor did the Allied high command.

Upon arrival of the replacement battalion the following day, the city was packed with GIs. The personnel staffs, or S1s, as they were called, were busy processing individual soldier pay requests and consolidating them with various tabs and charges of the local restaurants.

Along with the new supply battalion was a company of the 92nd Infantry Division out of Kansas. Despite their heroic feats and contributions in this war, it would be a Bob Marley song that made famous the Buffalo Soldiers. Not until Truman's administration, a few months ahead, would black soldiers be fully integrated into the armed services. For now, they still operated as segregated units.

Over the past few days, he enjoyed a hasty, mock Thanksgiving dinner with his men, and now it was finally December. Vic now could relax and enjoy ten days in the city before his battalion moved out to Poitiers to catch the bird that would drop them into northeastern France. He went to his favorite café, where Anso's friend, Chantelle, would serve him dinner. He enjoyed watching people cruise up and down the street with their baguettes and fresh fruits purchased at the local markets. Life was bubbling back up in the city that was nearly suffocated under Engel's iron fist. He saw some of the young black soldiers, polished from head to toe and walking in groups. They approached the café, where the leader of the group, a tall, broad-shouldered sergeant, flashed a grin at Chantelle, who blushed and smiled back. They made their way toward the café, until one them grabbed the sergeant from behind, discreetly pointing at Carlson. They all shot Carlson a quick glance and made a ninety-degree detour toward another café, a block down, where other black soldiers were dining.

"Why do you guys treat your own soldiers like that?" Chantelle complained as she scooped up Carlson's empty plate and glass.

Carlson looked at her in a confused manner, not comprehending her complaint.

"What do you mean, how we treat our own?" he asked.

"Making people eat separately from you because they are black. I am completely baffled by that behavior!" And she stormed off.

With Carlson's combined preoccupation with preparing his company to move out, and his anxiety at leaving Anso, he rarely noticed that the Buffalo Soldiers avoided him because they knew they were not permitted to share accommodations with white service members. Over the next few days, he would see the young sergeant with a bright smile walking hand in hand with Chantelle, as he would do with Anso. Sometimes, the young sergeant, whose name, Carlson learned, was Sergeant Grey, and Chantelle would join him and Anso, as they visited the park next to the river. Carlson was warned more than once by his first sergeant about being seen with a soldier from the "negro platoon" but ignored it. They were leaving in a few days anyway.

Eastern Belgium was a miserable place to be in the middle of December. Usually, digging a hole in the frozen earth to house three men would work up more than substantial energy and body heat.

Today, that strategy failed. The little bit of sweat Carlson and his men worked up only made them colder the second they stopped laboring. Upon completion, when they took their positions in the foxholes, dusk proved even worse. With a sinking sun and no physical labor, the men just sat there and froze. Yet tonight's paralyzing cold would not even scratch the surface of the horrors that await them.

Over a week ago, his unit had landed just south of Brussels and over the past days had marched down to vicinity of Liege, along the Meuse River. Like himself, and his superior, Lieutenant Colonel White, none of the strategists anticipated the Germans to be as audacious as to try to return through Belgium. Therefore, they scattered the 2nd Infantry Division throughout the Hurtzgen Forest on the Belgian and German border. Their mission was to go capture Heartbreak crossroads deep within the icy forest, blowing the Roer River dams, thus impeding access to the Muesse River and then to Antwerp. Behind the 2nd Infantry Division, as the untested 99th Infantry Division, who had yet to fire a weapon in combat, and Carlson's Regiment was right behind them, on the far end of the Elsenborn Ridge, the last line of defense.

Soon it would be dark, and the regimental commander would order his men in their holes for the evening. One man would sleep, and one would assume guard, in preparation for any repercussive outbreaks, as a result of the 2nd's movements. Sunset was just late afternoon in Belgium during the winter.

"Going to be a long night," Vic told his counterpart, as he sipped from his metal cup.

"It'll be a boring night!" Captain Aikin replied, taking a long puff on his cigarette.

"You don't think we will see anything?"

Aikin looked at him in disbelief and then shook his head. "Well, damn, Carlson! I mean, if there're enough Krauts out there to smash through two divisions, not a damn thing we are going to do about it! You intellectual types! You guys overthink taking a crap! You probably hold philosophical debates about whether to wrap toilet paper around your hand or fold it!"

Carlson knew that Captain Aikin could not stand him and thought him a snob. He looked over to see Lieutenant Colonel White walking the regimental commander through the area. Aikin stomped out his cigarette and looked at Carlson. They both made their way down the long trail to join their companies up front.

Time had never passed so slowly. Carlson spent a slow, excruciating eternity staring into a frigid, black abyss, pressing himself against the side of his snowy fox hole in a feeble attempt to generate warmth. He wanted and needed so bad to sleep, but the painful burning of his joints, due to the unbearable cold, prevented him. Out of boredom and to take his mind from his pain and discomfort, Vic began to notice the millions of stars in the sky that were only visible in a desolate rural area. They provided the only light in this very black, empty cold. How he wished something would lighten the landscape and warm his body. It was not the first time he regretted that for which he so desperately wished. His wish would be granted in the most diabolical and harrowing manner. He continued to tighten his body and press himself against the frozen ground of their hasty foxhole, he shared with his first sergeant, and private first class Pierson.

"Damn, sir, you are ready for the whole German army!" First Sergeant Lightfoot whispered, amused at his company commander hard pressed against his weapon aiming out into the dark.

Temperatures sank to two degrees Fahrenheit, frigid even for Belgium in that time of year, as an artic wind blasted through the region that winter. No way was Vic going to fall asleep as the cold paralyzed his limbs and sent pain scorching through his nerves.

When he felt a strong grip jerk his shoulder, there was no more intense pain from the cold. Again, a force jerking his shoulder, and now the intense pain returned. He then realized he was being awaken from what he thought was an impossible slumber.

"Sir, sir! I'm sorry, but, sir, wake up!" he heard Lieutenant Lemmon whisper. Still somewhat discombobulated, he looked over at his first sergeant, who silently pointed outward. Still surprised that he had been able to sleep, Carlson listened closely and heard the sound of gunfire and screams in German language emitting from the cold black abyss in front of him.

"Sir," Lieutenant Lemmon again whispered, "my platoon has exchanged fire with the Germans, and Zini's first platoon is completely engaged."

Carlson looked at him in disbelief.

"We are engaged, sir!"

"Roger, I heard you! Go back to your platoon. I will move up Dillingham's platoon and alert Aikin to get Bravo Company ready." He then turned to his first sergeant. "I guess Corps was right! There was going to be repercussions from 2nd ID taking those crossroads. But how did they get through a whole division?" he thought.

If the answer was not plainly obvious, the next twenty minutes would answer his question violently. The sounds of gunfire became more deafening. The distant cries of German commands were no longer distant, and the screams of men in his company now were close enough to make the hairs stand on his neck. It was no longer necessary to be keep noise discipline.

Irony is the incongruity between what would have been expected and what may have actually occurred. Morbid irony, however, is the fantastical expectation of the most dreadful, not realizing that this will become the actual reality. Only moments before, Carlson was wishing for something to break the sadistic silence, painful cold, and mind-numbing boredom. Only moments prior, Carlson was praying for something to lighten the abysmal darkness. Now, the landscape was so noisy and chaotic he could not hear himself scream. The frigid, sterilized air of the forest was choked with smoke; the sweet scent of fresh, burning pinewood contrasted with the smell of the hot steel of spent ammunition, and the stench of singed hair and burning flesh. *Irony.*

He sprinted toward his company as more blasts thundered around him, the crash of trees falling around him, momentarily stopping him in fear. After a series of more deafening shelling and rapid gunfire, he found a foxhole and jumped in there. It was not his, but someone was occupying it holding his rifle. Just as the helmeted head turned toward him, another harsh explosion lit up the whole area. Carlson saw that it was Staff Sergeant King, Dillingham's platoon sergeant.

"Goddamnit! Why in the hell have you guys not yet moved up toward Zini and reinforced First Platoon?! Answer me right now, goddamnit!" Carlson demanded, using a rare and uncharacteristic profanity, whose absence set him apart in a profession that used profane language as a custom.

King glared at him in disbelief. "Sir, Zini and his whole platoon are dead! There is not even one man to reinforce! The Krauts have his position. At this point, we are struggling just to hold this position!" Carlson was embarrassed and horrified that he had no idea what was happening to his own company and so shocked at how instantly the situation spiraled out of control. Even if he had time to register the fact that his key most effective lieutenant was dead, he would not have believed it. Zini was indomitable. Nothing ever seemed to bother him. When the rest of his company was wet, cold, and miserable, Zini not only did not seem to mind, but he also still felt free to fire off his brash and loud opinions. Now Zini, and his platoon of young twenty-year-olds who had matured years in only six months and who became the men who breached and liberated the small city in the Loire Valley, had now all instantly been killed in less than twenty minutes.

Rarely had Carlson ever really lost his composure. Perhaps it was part of his stern Southern upbringing, where a gentlemanly Southern figure never lost their composure or displayed sign of emotional distress, even in dire circumstances. Maybe it was just in his family, where he had never witnessed his father or his much older brother, Rubin, lose it. Nevertheless, after being blown out of the sky and injured while behind enemy lines, or near-brushes with death, marching west toward Bretagne, Carlson never showed any fear, sadness, or distress. However, tonight was different. He was a different man, screaming like a banshee and cursing. It was the only time he was completely out of control and had no idea what was happening or how it happened so quickly. Only an hour prior, he was literally in the dark, but now as the sky lit up like day, he was figuratively in the dark. Where did all these Germans come from? He then noticed that he was grabbing Sergeant King by the lapels of his drab-green service shirt. Something also uncharacteristic for Vic. He stared at King with disbelief, and with that, Sergeant King quickly hoisted himself out of the foxhole and sprinted toward the deadly chaos just yards ahead. Seeing his subordinate act so bravely compelled Carlson to do his best to harden his fear-stricken legs and do likewise, except Carlson had to run toward his first sergeant before he could move up to direct this suicidal battle. He could finally see his foxhole, but a series of rapid gunfire kicked up snow and pinecones just inches from his body and vibrated through his boots. He immediately hit the ground and crawled with his face buried in the snow.

"What nomenclature of weapon fires from that far away?" he wondered to himself. "Those Germans have to be at least a kilometer away." Unbeknownst to him, they were less than a hundred meters away.

By the time Carlson lifted his face out of the snow, he was at his foxhole, a new series of rounds popping up the snow in front him. He slid headfirst into his hole before he noticed that Pierson was in there screaming at him.

"Sir, Battalion sending the other companies and the attached 92nd company up this way!"

They were sending the whole battalion, plus two companies from the Buffalo Soldiers' division. Soldiers who just weeks ago were not allowed to dine alongside his men were now thrown into one of the fiercest battles of the Second World War to die alongside them in one of the first instances of racial segregation within the ranks.

Carlson's first sergeant was crouched down with his face buried between his knees. This was not the time for his top sergeant to break down mentally; he had to be out front leading, along with him. He pulled up his head by his hair and jumped back when he saw a light stream of smoke emitting from the sucking, bloody crater of what was once his gaunt and detailed face. He looked over to Lieutenant Lemmon's platoon and saw them being mowed down by German soldiers busting through brush, screaming. Paralyzed in shock, he watched every soldier in his third platoon drop in front of the flashing muzzles of the dark-coated figures screaming in German. Those not so lucky to be shot dead were bayonetted or their faces were smashed with rifle butts, as was done to Lieutenant Lemmon.

Flashing lights blinded Carlson, and the overwhelming daylight it produced betrayed Carlson and Pierson right there in their position, which was followed by a round of rapid fire, striking inches from his helmet, as he pathetically fired back in random directions. Carlson looked to his left and saw Aikin's men faring even worse. Carlson had to look away as Aikin's company was caught unaware and rendered helpless to German gunfire. If Aikin had trouble believing his counterpart Captain Carlson earlier that evening, a barrage of artillery shells that smashed through their position, shaking the ground, verified his counterpart's report. The blackened forest was now lit up like day, and Carlson did not even bother to crawl or maintain any light or noise discipline. He was now in the middle of an all-out battle.

It was time to die. Carlson was sure that Dillingham's second platoon had been wiped out just as easily. His orders were to wait for Lieutenant Colonel White, but dead men could not be punished, and Carlson did not want to live with the shame of being a commander seen alive while every man in his unit was dead. Before he could jump out of his hole and run headfirst into gunfire and artillery, he heard German voices just above him. Several of screaming soldiers fixed their rifles over Pierson and Carlson. Just as suddenly, dozens of holes exploded in their chests and stomachs, their falling bodies bruising Carlson as they landed on him, coughing up blood. Carlson looked to his left flank and saw the remnants of Aikin's destroyed company gunning down the Germans who had obliterated Carlson's company. Carlson looked behind him and saw dozens of soldiers whose dark faces were concealed in night that was untouched by German artillery. The muzzles from the guns they continued firing lit up their area, revealing them to be the Buffalo Soldiers who saved Carlson's life.

Carlson looked straight ahead and saw a massive, shadowy, almost animal-like figure slowly trample down the trees in its way. Carlson focused his vision in an attempt to make out what he was seeing or if he was hallucinating. When the last tree came crashing down, Carlson was stunned to see a German Panzer tank fixing its turret over his head. The crashing sound of the volley fired out exploded far off behind his position. It only occurred to Carlson a few seconds later that the remainder of the regiment was moving up to fight, and the Panzer tank had just immobilized them. Straight ahead to his right, Carlson saw another vehicle emerge, as it appeared over the embankment where his third platoon was positioned. The positioned gun on the vehicle let loose a burst of rounds that cut down the remainder of Aikin's company, and obliterated the ground around him and the now dead company. The Panzer tank screeched forward slowly and readjusted its aim. Carlson looked back over at the Buffalo Soldiers company and watched an exploding, massive ball of fire replace them as small pieces of fabric and debris flew outward from the raging fire.

Perhaps it was the multiple brain-busting blasts or simply fatigue. Whatever it was, Carlson felt drunk. He was present in the battle, but he was elsewhere. He felt the same lightheadedness as he did the night he consumed the wine back in the Loire Valley. Everything went in slow motion. He heard no more pounding but only an annoying buzzing. He felt several stings on his shoulder; then he couldn't feel his shoulder. Confused, he looked down at Pierson, with his blood-dripped hands, who was holding his throat from where blood was shooting two feet in the air, his eyes rolled into the back of his head. He then began to see black splotches, and he slowly felt himself go down, as though he were gently being lowered. Finally, some sleep! He deserved it.

He opened his eyes and immediately regretted it. Pain racked his shoulder and would have rendered him to tears, but his face was paralyzed. He heard voices and boots chomping the deep snow around him. Minutes went by before he realized he had participated in battle. He rolled over and saw his foxhole behind him. He saw his soldier Pierson with half his body lying out over the edge of the foxhole, his arms spread like angel wings, and his lifeless eyes staring up at the sky, and a gaping hole in his throat.

He began to hear whispering, "Sir, don't breathe too heavily!" He looked over to his left.

"Sir, control your breathing! The Germans can see the steam of your breath." Carlson's eyes were still blurry but after focusing, he saw that it was Dillingham. Dillingham had made it but looked bad.

The second time he came around, Carlson was a little more alert. He could now determine it was approximately midday. He remembered Dillingham's advice. He looked over toward him and stared directly into the lifeless eyes of Dillingham's limp, motionless body. Carlson's whole company was dead. He slowed to his breathing to a near stop and began to slide himself along the unforgiving, frozen turf. He stopped as he heard heavy breathing. Germans! Germans nearby and maybe even watching him. Except why just one person breathing? The breathing descended into uncontrolled sobbing. Carlson moved up and slithered through the charred ground, his body now covered in snow and ash. He looked up and saw one of the black soldiers crouched down, his face buried in his hands, crying. Around him were the crisply burned bodies of the rest of his company.

"Soldier! Hey!" Carlson whispered.

The soldier looked up, startled. Carlson was startled as well. He knew this soldier. It was Sergeant Grey, the young Buffalo Division soldier who courted Chantelle. They nestled up to each other for warmth. Grey buried his face in the captain's shoulder and cried uncontrollably. Later, when Grey had calmed down, they both continued to sit there, too exhausted mentally and spiritually to continue.

"You don't have a cigarette, do ya?" Grey asked.

"I don't. You guys should quit that habit...light and scent discipline!"

"Shit! Capt'n, that light discipline did us a shit load of good last night, didn' it?" Grey protested.

Carlson just looked at him.

"I guess I shouldn' talk to a white captain that way! Even if we do date the same French girls or shoot at the same Krauts!"

"Sergeant! There is no white and black, or officer and enlisted right now. You can address me any way you like! In a few hours, it won't matter. We will both be dead. And honestly, with this cold, I hope it's a quick German bullet that gets me!"

As the sun began to sink behind the thick trees of the Belgian forest, the frigid air and sound of German voices began to fill the night.

"We should take our positions, Sergeant! It was good knowing you!" And with that, he pulled Grey into the nearest foxhole, next to a dead member of Aikin's Company B. Carlson aimed his sidearm. He would take out at least one. The German voices grew louder as the activity grew closer. He could see the flashes of fire from distant muzzles. Loud bangs startled Carlson. Who was that close? Bullets whizzed by him, and he could see the silhouetted branches in dark explode. More shots rang out, and this time from *behind his position*. From his left, Carlson saw a whole company of soldiers spring up in unison and charge forward, discharging weapons in the cold evening as German commands now became frantic screams.

The Elsenborn Ridge was secured by the reinforcements.

Next time Carlson awoke, he was just miles near Liege, in a rear medical unit. His shoulder was bandaged, and he could not move it. An attendant forcefully lifted up the curtain to his tent.

"Captain! How is your shoulder healing?"

"Corporal. What is wrong with it?"

"Well, we had extract about four rounds out of your shoulder, two out of your leg. You will be on crutches for a little bit."

"Corporal, I need to see Lieutenant Colonel White, 5th Battalion Commander."

"Sir! He is dead, along with your Regimental Commander!"

Carlson sat there stunned.

"Sir, you're one of twenty-four surviving members of your entire regiment, and one of them is from the negro company." Carlson sat back, still in disbelief.

"Anyway, Captain, a liaison officer will be by next week to reassign you back to France, for recovery."

Carlson sat back and thought about his fellow company commander chiding him.

"Hell, Carlson, if there're enough Krauts out there to smash through two divisions, not a damn thing we are going to do about it!" he recalled.

Aikin's attempt to make Carlson's question sound stupid turned out to be one of the war's most accurate and macabre and ghoulish predictions.

Eisenhower drew the same assumption that Carlson and his superior had discussed that beautiful day in the Loire Valley. Hitler would be too preoccupied with the Russians converging on the east to give a second thought to retaking France. In fact, Hitler knew he was no match for the massive, merciless Soviet Red Army.

He desperately needed to reassemble his efforts in Western Europe and then turn around and defend from the Russians. Therefore, Hitler made one last desperate plunge into the Belgian border, overrunning Allied forces and driving them back so far he made a bulge into the Allied line, thus making this the *Battle of the Bulge* that would be one of the deadliest of the war, costing over 80,000 US casualties.

Carlson had to laugh at Aikin's factious remark, as there were in fact "enough Krauts to smash through two divisions," a quarter of a million Germans to be exact, accompanied by two divisions of Panzer tanks, and round after round of ground-shattering artillery. The early morning of December 16th, Carlson wondered how the Germans made it that far. In fact, so sure was the Allied command that Germans would not expand too much effort at the Belgian border, they spread out the 2nd ID upon tens of miles, leaving multiple gaps through which the Germans could easily slide. By the time the 2nd Infantry Division was able to engage them, the thousands of

Germans had surprised and were smashing the green, untested, unprepared, and surprised 99th Infantry Division. Thus, Aikin's smartass remark proved right. *Morbid irony.*

Weeks later in a Paris infirmary, when Carlson was fully recovered, he was granted a few days' leave. He took the first train from the Gare de Lyon south toward the Loire Valley. When he stepped out onto the train station, he saw a group of German prisoners all chained to each other being marched to the station. Carlson's eyes met with the young Nazi corporal who was briefly his driver. Over seventy years later, that driver would be here in the house Carlson had built for his family. *Morbid irony.*

Six

PENANCE

"I guess you have a point!" the old man, Karl, grins, showing off displaced black teeth, as smoke escapes from the gaps.

By now, our poor grandparents' porch is a cloud of smoke as Aunt Josie is smoking a roach, I fired up a cigar, and Frenz had hidden some filterless Camels that he was safe to smoke now that his overbearing son had retired.

"I am not sure that I should have even come by. I know I caused your family a lot of pain. But I had to, you understand!"

"Hey! No complaints here!" I reply, pouring myself another drink and not knowing what to say exactly, "Personally, I don't know why anyone cares. I mean if you are soon to be—" I stop, realizing what I said. As usual, the alcohol made the words escape faster than my thoughts could impede them.

"It's okay! I am soon to be dead! I mean, Christ, kid, look at me! I look like the cast of *The Walking Dead*! Only that I am not walking!" He grins as he snuffs out his cigarette and pours himself another straight scotch.

Part of me envies his apathy. I have always been a runner and practiced some jujitsu. I exercise regularly and even feel guilty about my mass alcohol intake. I envy Old Man Frenz's ability to not even care that he can't walk, is two steps away from death, and still sucks down Camels and booze with reckless abandon.

Aunt Josie inhales and holds her breath. A slight cough follows, then a question. "So, why did you come here? I mean, you told us, sure. But why did you have to see our grandmother once more? Did you love her?"

Old Man Frenz take another sip of his drink and just stares off for a second.

"You know, I realize you think it was wrong for me to come here. But remember this. Your grandparents probably lived a wonderful life together. Of course, it was marred by the sinister history they shared, the dehumanizing circumstances under which they met, and the secrets of utter horror they kept not only from you but from each other, and even worse, tried to bury within themselves. But as I look at your aunts and uncles, and I look at this house, and hear about your grandfather's legacy as a civil rights' attorney, you have to say they did well despite. I mean, everyone seems content except for you!" He points at me with a trembling finger. "His oldest grandson."

He has a good point that totally escaped me, as even in my lightheaded state, I notice something. He refers to me as *his* grandson. My grandmother confided in me only a few years ago that my father was actually Frenz's son, as she was only weeks pregnant when Carlson's company liberated the city. Frenz does not know that he is talking to his true grandson.

"Yes, your grandparents did well. I cannot say the same for myself."

Penance is the confession of sin, made with sorrow and with the intention of amendment, followed by penitential discipline.

Karl Frenz

Very few of us who fought with the Germans were really Nazis. Many were Eastern Europeans like me who simply found ourselves governed by a powerful Germany that so rapidly swallowed us up, we actually thought we were Germans.

I was born just after the Bolshevic revolution overthrew the Russian czar who had ruled over Russia for close to a thousand

years. By the time I was born in 1920, the world was already in cha-
otic turmoil. The world was engulfed in a deadly pandemic. World
War I had ended badly for the Austrians, but worse for Germans,
whose sole sin was simply siding with Austria, in opposition to
France, who had allied with the Russians, Germany's adversary.
Two mighty, thousand-year empires collapsed as they had sided
with the central powers against the Allies in the Great World War.
They were the Ottomans from Turkey, who controlled most of the
Middle East, and North Africa. The other one was the Austrian-
Hungary Empire, a constitutional remnant of the great Hapsburg
family who at once ruled Spain, the Netherlands, all of what is to-
day Central America, and most of what is South America, and the
Phillipines, named for one of their monarchs, King Phillip of Spain,
as well as controlled most of Italy.

Britain mercilessly punished the Ottoman Turks, who also
made the bad decision of allying themselves with Austrians and
the Central Powers. The Ottomans' defeat resulted in the complete take over and divide of the Ottoman controlled nations of the
Middle East. Winston Churchill perfectly carved up Turkey's Middle
East so as to pit them, hostile, against each other. Part of Persia, or
what is today Iran, was carved into today's Iraq so that there would
always be a Shi'a Islamic culture in what was undoubtedly Sunni
Islamic Arabic culture.

The fallout was not as bad for Eastern Europe, but a fallout,
nonetheless. Two years before I was born, the Austrian-Hungary
Empire collapsed, and from it, many different ethnic factions broke
off and declared themselves independent countries. Among them,
Czechoslovakia, Serbia, Croatia, and my country, Hungary, all lands
from where the Hapsburgs had pushed out the Ottomans centuries
before and had claimed as their own.

The extreme change of events, compounded with Germany's
plunging hopeless depression, destabilized all of Eastern Europe.
You found work where you could and remained there regardless
the cruel, inhumane circumstances. My father worked eighteen
hours a day at a factory and pounded down vodka when he was

not working. Clear grain alcohol, frigid temperatures, and hours of manual labor had shriveled the old man's face, making him look decades older.

I was five years old by the time my sister was born. By 1925, Lenin had died, and his October Revolution had manifested into a centralized controlled economy under his successor, a man whose name would strike fear into millions throughout the world, Joseph Stalin. Stalin's Red Army not only forcefully imposed his rigid form of Communism on these now territories, but he also established forces to purge and destroy any suspected opposition. Stalin had single-handedly crushed Transcaucasian and Byelorussian and then by infiltration put down any hopes of the Ukrainian people establishing their own Ukrainian Republic for which they had so hoped after the dispose of the czar.

By the time Europe was overly concerned about the threat this spreading ideology, in 1933, I was thirteen and caring for a sister who, at ten years old, had just been stricken with polio. A year later, her paralysis had confined her to a wheelchair, and this was my mother's breaking point. My father's drunken beatings and my sister's condition led to her nervous breakdown. In 1930s Hungary, there were no immediate twenty-four-hour hotlines. Psychiatric help had the prestige of black magic, sorcery, and fortune telling. No mercy existed for those whose fragile mentalities and sensitive emotions had collapsed under the impossible life of yesteryear. They were just labeled "crazy" or referred to as "one of *them*." Two men came and simply took her away as she looked nearly comatose. I tried helplessly to stop them and part of me left with her. I loved my mother and felt helpless as I watched these two cold strangers drag her away, leaving me to the unforgiving mercy of a drunk, oft violent father. When those two heartless men took away my wonderful, caring, loving mother, my only supernumerary was my aunt and my sister.

In the absence of my mother's kindness, my older brother and I had to fend for ourselves. My brother took a job as my father's alcoholism hardened its relentless grip over him. My aunt and I cared for my sister, Dora. Despite her debilitating condition, her attitude was always beyond phenomenal. After close to ninety years, I can honestly say that I would never have made those dark, cold, passionless years in 1930s Hungary but for my sister's illuminating spirit. She did not inherent the pale, shriveled features of the Frenz family as had cursed my brother and me, but she had my mother's white, flawless skin and pleasantly contrasting black hair. Each time I arrived back from the local grocery or from school, she would maneuver her wheelchair my way and greet me with a cheering smile.

For the next years after my mother's commitment to the mental institution, and my father's subsequent death, and our resulting eviction, Dora's illuminating spirit was the safety net from all of our descending decadence into a bottomless pit. Half of my adolescent memories consisted of the beautiful face of my sister, her flowing black hair and her graceful posture in the face of polio, economic hopelessness. I would go to school, return, and in turn, teach her what I had learned. I taught Dora guitar, English, and French, and how to do algebraic equations. When I turned seventeen, my nineteen-year-old brother had lost his job, as was the case with many helpless people in that time. My brother then enlisted in the German army. Not knowing what to do, and lacking any creativity, I did the same.

By the late 1930s, most of Hungary, frightened from the possibility of Stalin's spread of Communism, had turned to Germany. Many thought Hitler was a crank but never thought he would have any type of future in a country like Germany that valued precision and pragmatism. Many realized that only someone as crazy as Hitler was the only hope of stopping a growing militant Communist cancer that was rapidly swallowing up our continent. We were not alone. Romania, who initially swore neutrality, eventually joined Germany, as did many citizens from Czechoslovakia. Although, like Poland, in less than two years, they would have no choice as Hitler would swallow up those countries effortlessly, just as he did Greece, Serbia, Croatia, and the remainder of those newly formed countries that were but remnants of the fallen Austrian empire. Hitler was going to reconfigure the Hapsburg Empire in his own distorted, depraved image, but under Prussian rule, not Austrian. In doing so, it would be the only thing to thwart the Soviet advance. Penance.

Like my father, my brother was never one for emotion, when it was time to leave. He walked out the door with zero attachment or connection. He left with zero regret for the family he was leaving behind. I, conversely, felt the sting of leaving my aunt and especially my sister, Dora. As miserable as life was here, it pained me to leave it, and I looked soft as compared to my steely-eyed brother. The hard years had forged our bond, made us a team. I worried about how my aunt would fare taking care of my sister without me. However, most of my pain was selfish and less altruistic. I missed my sister. Together we made the horrific and unbearable bearable. While many in my country turned to alcohol, we had each other's company. I was never meant to be a soldier, you see, but life in those times left no such option.

Many of the Nazi rank within the Storm Trooper Brigade that oversaw basic training agreed that I was never meant to be a soldier. Nonetheless, they witnessed and appreciated my knack for secretarial skills and gift for languages. They transferred me to a Wehrmacht unit as opposed to a front-line Storm Trooper unit. I was assigned to a Berlin headquarters transmitting documents for a year and half. After that, I caught the attention of a rising colonel, who assigned me to one of his sturm commanders who was to command one of the thousands of occupied cities.

I was impressed by Major Engel. Never had I met a more direct, candid, and to-the-point individual and to this day have yet to meet one. With most people, mind games are essential. Yet, with Engel, you knew where you stood. So engrained was I in the daily grind of intimate personal details of Nazi life, it was a couple of years before I learned of their heinous atrocities. Friends from Hungary and Czechoslovakia penned me letters describing the swastika armband robot like soldiers that corralled their Jewish neighbors into waterless ghettos without electricity. I read the letter but failed to believe them. These could not be my comrades in arms. I knew in my heart that such a standup officer like Major Engel would never approve of such inhuman atrocities.

Eventually, the hard truth of my existence slowly seeped into me. After time, I began learning the truth of their harrowing accusations. I often overheard Strobel discussing how is old unit would round up Jewish people for relocation to the European ghettos. I began to oversee the publication of anti-Jewish propaganda to be displayed in all territories controlled by the Germans. By then, it was too late. The ends had justified the means. Maybe waterboarding would be good to prevent another 9/11. No matter. Hitler was only disposing of Communists, and so what if he disposed of a few Jews or Gypsies in the process? So what? This question would be painfully answered as I was not only personally witness to the atrocities but complicit in them. Later, I would be tasked with cleaning up an atrocity of which I was a shameful part. It would only be the beginning of the penance life would cast upon me for my part in such systematic evil. It would be a penance that began with the cleanup and would be highlighted by the loss of your grandmother.

When I first met Anso, I was ordered by Engel to go to her store and have her father, Monsieur Chevalier, construct a custom-made frame to accommodate a seven-foot portrait of the fuehrer. She was curt and disrespectful. I could not blame her. We were occupying their city.

"You know how that is?" Frenz winks at me. "Those Afghanis loved you, I am sure!"

"Karl, we did not have even a fraction of the liberties with the Afghan locals that you seemed to have had, Gramps!" He goes silent, but I am not sure if he caught the "Gramps" comment, or if he thinks I am being my usual disrespectful self.

I kept seeing Anso as I went about my daily errands for the major. The moment she caught my attention was when she was wheeling her brother, Thomas, into one of the few restaurants we left for the locals. She would brush his hair back and move his plate up for him. The image made me homesick, and I longed for my family again. I even thought of my calloused brother, whom the Germans had recruited for front-line battle that had suited someone of his raw, tough demeanor. I could tell that Anso seemed to enjoy his company and did not mind at all the inconveniences that may come with caring for someone in such a state. I could see a genuine aura of enjoyment to have her brother in her company, very much unlike Mademoiselle Benoit, who seemed to have a look of shame and exhaustion when escorting her little Adrienne throughout town. It takes a certain type of patience and love to deal with people's disadvantages. When the polio had poor little Dora at the worst, I would help her eat and to the bathroom. I never minded. I saw the same patience in Anso. She never seemed to mind helping little Tomas. Like the bond between Anso and her best friend, Genevieve; ours was also forged by the struggle of having to care for a disadvantaged loved one and the pain shared in doing so.

When Captain Strobel first issued the order to round up known homosexuals, I did not care. I thought they were perverts anyway. When the order was issued to round up known Communists, I thought likewise. This was, after all, whom we were fighting. Again, with the Jews, they probably had it coming regardless, those thieves. Yet when the order was published to round up those with disabilities, I could not believe it.

Were we really this inhumane?

I did not believe we were capable of such and figured it was just Strobel exaggerated our duties to his own sick means. I snuck into Engel's office and searched the files that I had shuffled multiple times that day. After thirty minutes, my heart sank into my stomach. I saw the official order from our higher headquarters to euthanize those who were deemed handicapped. I was fortunate enough not be one of the soldiers tasked with pulling children who were literally clinging from their parents but heard the ghastly stories nonetheless, as stories traveled fast in that small town. I no longer wanted to be seen by the townspeople, your grandmother especially, I was so ashamed. I was going to end my life. How did I end up a party to something to depraved and base? No matter, I would take my side arm and that evening drink up and blow my brains out.

Engel could find another clerk just as easily, and death had become so common anyway, it would be no big deal. Once again, nothing was noble about what I was doing. I was not going to end my life from guilt at the pain I was inflicting on innocent townspeople. I was ending my life because I could not bear to be witness to this any longer. I no longer wanted to be a part of something that would hurt people like Dora.

But what if I instead did something to stop it? After all, any and all administrative matters came through me. That would even be worse as I would be acting in a traitorous manner. Or maybe I could just save a few. Nobody would notice that. Maybe just Anso's brother.

Anso began to warm up to me after I saved little Thomas. In the months following, I would treat her to lunch. I would tell her about Dora and my older brother, although I did not mention he was a front-line Storm Trooper, or SS. Anso told me about Genevieve and all the animals she cared for before we invaded her city. It was one of the best years of my life. It was a year I could forget that I served with Wehrmacht and I could be human again. I knew that year would not last. I knew I had my penance coming for my association with the Nazis. I wanted to share this year with Anso in every way I knew how. But the best year of my life was the worst year of hers.

The following year, in 1943, the German war effort was ramped up tenfold, as the entrance of the United States and Russia had vastly overwhelmed Hitler's forces. Casualties increased exponentially, and the demand for resources drained most occupied cities. Soon, most business shut down altogether, and those that miraculously survived were solely for German use only and with the French being rationed what little we would permit them. From the end of 1943 to mid-1944, I would still see Anso but not regularly. I would sneak items to her family that most French had been deprived for over a year. At this point, I was praying that the Allies would hurry up and finish this war. Always be careful for what you wish. In November of that year, my wish came true and thus the first day of a decade-long nightmare.

I still recall vividly when Carlson's company invaded the city we held. I remember it, not because of the event itself. By the time Captain Carlson's company attacked the city, our unit was already defeated and demoralized. The writing was on the wall. Half of us were happy to surrender and ready to beg the Americans to take us prisoner, lest the Russians do. It was on Major Engel's stubborn insistence that we fight to the death, and so they did. The Americans punished our unit's leadership for their resistance, and Engel was defiant and insistent to the very end, even polishing up before being shot. I remember it for different reasons. I remember the last time I visited Anso.

I was sneaking some meat, wine, and cigarettes to her family. Normally, I would pace up and down her street, looking at a blank piece of paper and occasionally peering at address numbers, as though I were on an errand for the major. I would simply stroll up and down the street until one of the Chevaliers saw me, and they would wait for me to pass their door. Once I was squarely in front of the door, they would open it, and I would quickly sidestep in to deliver their goods. This time Anso opened. Once I was inside, I made my announcement.

"Hey, Anso! How are you holding up?" I asked.

"Good, good" she said in an uncharacteristically soft voice. "I vomited again this morning," she informed me, this time with a tone of worry in her voice as she held her lower stomach. The gesture to me was clear. She was pregnant with your father.

"Look, I have a plan, Anso! We need to get out of here tonight!"

It was difficult enough to talk up the courage, but seeing the doubt and hesitation in her eyes only demoralized me further.

"We need to get out of here tonight! I mean, how long can we do this? Eventually, someone will catch us! I will be fired from my post, imprisoned, and possibly shot. I certainly will no longer enjoy the major's protections, and that will be the best scenario. I do not want to think of the worst!" I pleaded.

"Karl! I don't know! I mean, what do you want me to do? Leave with you? And do what? I mean, your attention that you have paid our family has already cost us the friendship of every other townsperson who hates us for accepting any gifts from the Nazis!" Anso pleaded back, "I mean, don't mistake me, we greatly appreciate what you did for us, it's just that—"

"I am not a—" But she interrupted me before I could plead with her that I was not one of them, the Nazis.

"Oh, stop with that, Karl! You *are* one of them! And what are we going to do? How are we going to keep running? The Germans have the whole European continent under their grip!"

"No! No, they don't! They are losing their grip more and more each day. The Allies are closing in on them from all directions! The Americans from the north, the British from south, and the Russians from the east; this city is one of few that the Germans are still holding. Most of them are scurrying back to Germany in complete disarray! This is our perfect chance! We can leave tonight and make it down to Nice. You and your family can see Thomas again."

She did not have to say anything. I knew the answer when I saw the tears in her eyes. However, I never knew it would be my last chance to run away with her, and I certainly had no idea that it would be my last time with her ever. It was the last time I saw her until tonight.

When the Americans took over the city, they were rowdy and boisterous. Carlson allowed his soldiers to run wild, grope the girls, and get obnoxiously drunk. Engel would have killed us for this behavior. Another thing that amazed me was that when the black unit arrived, they were made to eat in separate restaurants from the white soldiers. I remember a friend of Anso, her name was Chantelle, was courted by a young black man. Once his unit took off with Carlson's unit, no white soldier would ever so much as look at her. She was an outcast among the Americans. The Americans treated their own soldiers like that, but *we were* the bad guys.

They treated young black men who had, just like them, been willing to give up their lives, as subhuman, yet they castigated us for our treatment of Jews and Communists. It was one of many dark ironies that cast their shadow over Europe as the war loomed toward its cataclysmic conclusion.

Once Captain Carlson had successfully taken over the city, the captain had imprisoned every enlisted man but made me his personal aide for my ability to speak English, French, and German. I painfully watched as the new commander, whose boots I now shined, court a girl with whom I had fallen madly in love. And he was gone just as quickly. I then rejoined my unit in the local jailhouse, where I shared a cell, toilet, and floor with five other German soldiers, who once enjoyed gallivanting the streets above and dined each night in the best of the city's restaurants. Now we were degraded to bread and water, and the ridiculing taunts of the supply battalion, who had never seen action but enjoyed acting as though they did.

A senior officer pulled me aside and threw me into my own cell.

"Hey! The colonel has some questions for you!"

A sharply uniformed man, whom I assumed was a senior officer, with a silver oak leaf on his hat, entered the cell, and the door closed behind him.

"Now, I understand that you speak English, is this correct?"

"It is." I nodded in cooperation.

The colonel looked over at an enlisted soldier who was hurriedly scribbling everything that I said.

"Prisoner, my name is Lieutenant Colonel George Holcomb, and I am the battalion commander for the 402nd Quartermaster Battalion. Our battalion, as I am sure you are aware, replaced the 5th Battalion that had taken this city. Now I am going to ask you some questions, do you understand?"

I nodded my head.

"What was your position in your unit?"

"Sir, I was an admin assistant to the commander."

"Okay, did your commander actually engage US troops, upon Company C's arrival?"

"Sir, I do not know. I was in the office when the city was taken!"

"So, you have no idea how your boss, Major Engel, was shot in the head at close range?"

"Sir, as I said, he was already killed when the hotel de ville was surrounded," I lied.

"Well, that is funny. I have heard"—he paused and peered over his glasses, at his assistant's notes—"I have heard, now, fourteen different versions of how your commander was killed, from prisoners and townspeople alike!" He paused and stared at me over the thick rims of his pointed glasses.

Long awkward seconds slowly passed, as I remained silent, and the colonel simply continued to stare at me out of the rim of his glasses, until finally, I felt compelled to say something, lest the colonel and I remain there for eternity, staring at each other.

"Sir," I mumbled, clearing my throat in a hopeless effort to sound more assertive, "I think the reason you hear so many stories, is because everything was so confusing. It was the heat of battle. You probably would have no idea, sir," I continued condescendingly, taking notice to see if he had picked up on my mocking his from behind the desk, administrative, lack of combat experience,

"but in combat scenarios, when men are fighting for their lives, fully aware that any minute the lights could go out, people's adrenaline are mind-numbing. Actually, there is no such thing as a mind. People's minds turn off, and mechanical instinct takes over. If men were still subject to their minds, they would be frozen and paralyzed in fear. I realize, sir, that you heard fourteen different stories, and I can assure you that each soldier that told you their account, recited it just as they remember it. But the key here, as *they remembered* it, in the midst of anarchy and confusion. I am telling you he was already dead and dragged out of the building that the unit you had replaced had surrounded. Knowing Major Engel, and do rest assured, I knew him better than anyone, he probably had one of his soldiers trapped in the building with us shoot him right in between the eyes. Engel was beyond proud, and there was no way he was going to be regulated to sharing a cell with his own soldiers while being interrogated by someone like yourself! Honestly, I am surprised he did not have me shoot him. It was I who did everything for him, ran every errand. I was his personal assistant, and toward the end, when things began to appear more dire and hopeless, I was truly one of the few people he spoke to. But make no mistake. I know he had someone shoot him at close range. It was the only way he was going out of that building. Again, sir, with all respect, I do not believe you could possibly understand. Hence why you will never believe any story told about his death, no matter how varied they may be!"

He lifted up his head but kept his eyes fixed on me above the rim of those glasses. I could easily tell that he had picked up on my snide comments, mocking his lack of combat experience, and I could just as easily tell he was irritated, if not enraged over the slight.

"Well, that sounds great!" the colonel finally said as he peered down at his notebook he had just angrily slammed shut. "Well, then! I suppose I have no choice but to believe you, the *combat soldier*!" I detected *his* sarcasm, "But you know, Corporal, we are the enemy, and so was Captain Carlson when he took your city. So, I must ask, why are you so insistent on protecting Carlson? Tell me!"

"Sir, I am not protecting anybody, especially you dirty Americans! I honestly did not—"

"Okay, okay! We are done here!" he said, discouraged.

None of the high command understood. We *despised* staff soldiers who could so easily and zestfully prosecute those actually fighting in the field.

"Sit tight, Frenz, I may have a job for you," the colonel said when he returned, and thus left me in my own private cell, a luxury I no longer took for granted. Penance.

My last night in the cell, a ray of fluorescent light broke the peaceful darkness where I hid from my captors. I looked up out of my half slumber to see Anso standing there with an awkward grimace, knowing she was somewhere forbidden.

"A friend of mine works with the Americans! They allowed me in, but I can't stay long! I brought you something!" And she produced out her bag, a fresh baguette, and some choice meat. Another luxury I had taken for granted. "My family figured it was the least we could do."

She handed me the items, and our hands met. If I could, I would have held on for eternity.

"Karl, I am sorry about—"

"Don't worry, Anso! I just want you and your family to be happy."

"I never meant to be in that jeep with the captain. It's just, I had to see Genevieve's house one last time. I will never forget you, and I hope you get to see your sister again."

I knew they were going to kill me though.

I watched her turn away and close the door behind her, and the pitch-black darkness descended upon me in her absence. I broke down and cried in the darkness where, thankfully, nobody could see me. Our commonalities in caring for a disabled family member were not the only thing that bonded us but two people trying to ascertain who they were in a world that had spiraled into chaos. Seeing her go was unbearable, and I was glad to know that soon I would be put out of my misery by the Americans.

I knew that I would never see her again. I loved her. The time we spent together brought normality to those bizarre years that would eternally change the course of the entire world. Yet I realized that while these were some of the best years of what was my sad, pathetic life, these were the worst years of what I later learned was otherwise a good life for her. The young, headstrong French woman, who would move to America to marry a judge, a former civil rights attorney, would do anything to forget such a harrowing time.

The next day they marched me out, along with some other prisoners who had a particular skill the Allies found useful, be it radio expertise, mechanical aptitude, or languages. We were marched in unison, ordered to walk in step, as a sergeant called cadence. Out of the corner of my eye, I saw Anso looking at me, but I didn't want to look. I was ashamed to be seen this way. I was ashamed to be in this war. I was ashamed to be alive and be me. We approached the train station and ordered to halt. When the train finally arrived, Captain Vic Carlson, limped off, visibly injured. I knew I had lost Anso. I had mourned for her last night and would continue to do so, while the train carted me away to indefinite imprisonment.

I wanted to say that I was jealous. After all, the captain who had made me his driver and servant got to return and take one of the only women I had ever loved. Carlson got to return worry free to be with a woman with whom I had spent a few years that spanned an eternity in my life, and meanwhile I got to be shipped off to what God only knew was going to be a hellish punishment for the punishment I had helped inflict on the world. I wanted to be angry. Yet the truth was, I was too tired, too defeated, and most of all, too frightened at the fate which awaited me to be angry.

Carlson and I would meet again.

Due to his impressive record leading a company through France and defending the Belgian border against Hitler's deadly plunge, and due to his debilitating injury rendering him useless as an infantry officer, he was promoted to major and assigned to be an aide to a three-star general who worked as Eisenhower's chief of staff. I, along with other prisoners, was tasked with cleaning up a devastated European infrastructure. Spending most of the war protected under the light task of paperwork that permitted me the luxury of remaining in one place and not seeing real combat until Carlson took the city, I had taken for granted the shear destruction we had wrought upon Europe.

I had never been an athletic figure. Yet the long hours I spent hoisting stone and other debris that German artillery and shelling that caused to spill in what were once brilliantly architected French streets broke me down physically. Many days, I had wished for anything to break up the dreadful tasks of cleaning up these cities. Always be careful what you wish for.

Four months after I boarded that train, the Germans surrendered when Berlin was crushed in between US and British from the west and the Soviets from the east. Germany was now completely under Allied control. Once the Allies had successfully ridded all of Europe of Nazi occupation, one by one, Allies stumbled upon and freed concentration camps. I had wished for something to take me away from cleaning up the streets, and now I had to clean up the piles of bodies that barely resembled anything human, but contorted figures of flesh, lifeless eyes popping out fragile skulls, wrapped in bulging blood vessels. Every soldier who encountered the site immediately vomited, and I did as well. So disastrous was this scene that word went all the way up to the supreme Allied commander, General Dwight Eisenhower. As we were loading rotting corpses and swatting away the flies they attracted, a procession of vehicles with flags bearing four stars pulled into the camp.

"Keep working! Keep working! Nobody told you to stop!" a soldier shouted, as everyone else in the camp abruptly stopped and waited for the door of the vehicle to open.

Carlson came out, holding the chief of staff's backpack on his shoulder, and carried a small notebook on which to take notes on what was mentioned by any dignitary that may have been present in which to review with his boss later. Carlson quickly moved around to open the door for a general who slowly emerged out of the vehicle. Immediately, the general held his nose and grimaced. Upon regaining his composure, he slowly looked around. The look of disgust on his face grew more disdained. Another line of jeeps entered the camp, and the crowd around this procession was bigger than the original. Cameramen were snapping photos at the man who slowly stepped down off of the jeep. I had never imagined the commander of the Allies to be such a skinny, short, old-looking guy. Carlson followed dutifully behind the three-star who approached Eisenhower, saluted him, and led him around the field. I kept loading the bodies, exhausted from having held my breath and performing labor. Sudden movements startled me, and in my fatigue, it took me a while to figure out what had erupted. Eisenhower had grabbed one the prisoners by his collar and shouted at him, "See what you did! This is what you did!" He looked back and indicted a crowd of townspeople who stood there in tearful awe under the disapproving gaze of British and US soldiers. He never said it to me personally, but I realized that I was the target of it. Even though I had never once traveled to Germany before my eighteenth birthday and had less in common with these townspeople then the general who bared their name or the very recently deceased President

Roosevelt, who had spent his childhood there, I may as well have been their family. As far as they were concerned, I was German.

I spent the next five years in prisons and labor camps throughout Britain. German POWs captured before the surrender, and those captured upon surrender, were assigned into forced labor programs under the Treaty of Yalta. Germans were forced into labor all throughout Europe. I was one of the fortunate ones, I was taken to Britain, and I have Carlson to thank.

I lied when I said I never contacted your grandmother out of her happiness. I respected your grandfather because I felt as though I owed my life to him. Yes, he stole away Anso, but he also made sure I was assigned to a British work camp. Germans imprisoned elsewhere did not fare so well. In Czechoslovakia, those Germans who were not expelled altogether were forced to wear bands, as they had once made their Jewish victims. In France, they were punished severely for the humiliation they had imposed on the French for those five years. German prisoners there were forced to clear mines in Verdun.

The last I had heard of my brother, he had gone to a Soviet work camp. I never heard from him nor heard anything about him since. Many Germans shot themselves rather than be captured by the Soviets or went out in a blaze of glory, dashing toward their captors, making their imminent deaths faster and less tortuous.

In 1949, the worst decade of my life, a decade made bearable only by Anso, had ended, and I was released from forced labor. I opted to remain in Britain, one of the few countries that permitted former German prisoners to remain there indefinitely. I found odd jobs and labor where I could and soon joined a company that taught me trades. It was a far cry from the brainy, administrative pencil work to which I had grown all too accustomed, but it was work, and I was no longer in prison.

Throughout the war, I would receive letters from my sister and my aunt, who was caring for her in my absence. During my incarceration, I had no real address but sent her letters whenever I could. Finally, I was a free man once again. I had a small, dingy, dirty apartment, but an apartment with a mailing address. Dozens of letters would come rolling in, some dated as far back as three years prior. My eyes welled up with tears, as I would read her desperate pleas for response: "It has been months since I have heard from you,; are you okay? Where are you? When will you write? You are becoming like your brother! We have not heard from him for close to a year, but he is on the front line."

We started corresponding regularly once again, and finally in 1957, I decided to go to the Hungarian consulate and renew my passport to reenter my home country. I had also applied for residency in the United Kingdom but wanted to remain a citizen in my home country.

I traveled to Paris and then took a long train ride to Hungary. I expected to travel all the way to Budapest, but upon arriving on the Hungarian border, the train stopped. The doors opened, and two Soviet soldiers boarded; an icy glare sized up the travelers on board. They checked every document, passports, and train tickets, items that had nothing to do with travel or rightful presence within the country. Nothing was exempt from their hard scrutiny.

Most of the passengers were herded off of the train, as we either had tickets that indicated a city in Hungary as our final destination, or a Hungarian passport, or both. Once off the train, we were lined up in single file outside an imposing chain-length fence that towered over the beautiful fields that used to be my country. In front of the entrance to this gate was a long table, where two Communist officials sat. One was interviewing the unsuspecting passengers. He was a short, stocky man with a red beard and steely eyes that pierced each person he interviewed as he peppered them with questions, looked down to scribble down quick notes, and collected their passports. On each side of the table stood two soldiers, dressed sharply in a long, gray uniform, adorned in red, with a shiny red cap that came down over their eyes that stared straight ahead. Rifles were slung across their backs.

My country was now Soviet-style Communist. It claimed to be its own government but was merely a puppet of Moscow, as was

Poland, Czechoslovakia, and Yugoslavia. One by one, countries to the east of Berlin fell like dominoes under Stalin's icy grip and disappeared behind his iron walls that would silence them for the next fifty years. Everything I feared was now unleashing its horrific tentacles in front of me. Aligning myself with the monsters that were Engel and Strobel, turning a blind eye to the century's worst atrocities, was all for the purposes of stopping the one man I feared more than Hitler, more than the devil, and he now ran my country in ruthless dictatorship. History is in fact written by the victors, and the victors would tell you that Hitler was the worst villain in history. Everyone we don't like is compared to Hitler. Hitler came to embody any and all evil, and once people crossed a certain threshold of depravity, be they Saddam Hussein or Mommar Quadaffi, they lost their human identity and now simply became "like Hitler."

But to the Eastern Europeans, who when the time came, chose Germany over Soviet Russia, Stalin represented an evil even more ruthless. Because he was the victor, rarely will his atrocities be discussed. Although the animalistic behavior of the Red Army is documented, it is buried under the more voluminous accounts of Nazi depravity. We are not only educated but inundated with accounts of the Auschwitz death camp in southern Poland. Almost never is it taught about the liberators who once they chased the Nazis out, brutally raped the survivors, and when rape was not enough, they chewed their already sickly flesh. Soviet-style Communism was a slavery we feared, and rightfully so. Our failure to stop it in the war resulted in over half the world falling under its cruel bondage. From behind the Berlin Wall, throughout Eastern Europe, to Maoist China, where over ten million people were killed for being suspected opposition, to Korea, Vietnam, throughout most of Asia, throughout the Central and South Americas. Communism was slavery. It was a system that owned your work, your products, and your produce you cultivated on their collective farms. It owned your property, and its intolerance knew no bounds. Any mere suspicion of opposition warranted your disappearance. No trials were implemented, no questioning a statement, or even bothering to double-check an accusation. The accused was visited by state police in the middle of the night and never seen again.

It was now my turn to stand in front of the desk. The intimidating stares from the soldiers melted me and stripped me of any courage or humanity. The woman in front of me was still being questioned. Her passport was jerked out of her hand by the man at the table and with a jerk of his head, silently motioned for her to pass through. The passport was tossed in a basket with other passports.

I had thought I had paid my dues for my involvement with the Nazis. How naive was I to think that my semi-comfortable work camp that eventually offered me British residency would be adequate reparation for my crimes. How stupid was I to think that my servitude under the gentlemanly Major Carlson would make up for little Adrienne, or the Bourgeois family. No, sir, my real prison sentence was just about to begin and would be forever. This was my penance. I was going to learn what it was like to be those poor French citizens that squirmed under constant watchful eye of Engel and suffered under unforgiving iron fist of Strobel, who scooped up opposition on whim.

The man who stared me down and demanded my passport was the new Engel, and I was the poor French townsperson who now had to relent to his heartless robotic soldiers. I looked over the head of the steely-eyed man and saw my sister after over ten years. Any fear, frustration, or sorrow was completely erased with her real image. Many years, her simple letters were enough to keep me going. She had not changed in ten years. Her peaceful smile still lifted me. Meanwhile, my years in the German army and subsequent imprisonment had aged me beyond my years. The look of joy in her face meant everything to me, and I felt content as she wheeled herself up to the fence. But the fence. I looked up beyond her and fixated on the jagged barbed wire that curled over the fence.

"I will need your passport, sir!" the man demanded, as he looked up at me with a smug look. I looked down at him, and then looked back up at Dora, whose joyous look now turned to consternation.

I backed away from the table. I felt like a force not generated by me moved me away. Dora's face grew more confused. I quickly spun around and rushed to the train station to purchase a return trip to Paris. I wanted to be as far away from that table as possible. In doing so, I abandoned my sister behind that sinister, imprisoning wall. The last look I remember on her face was that horrified look when she realized I would never pass through those gates and never again be in her life. Dora lost both of her brothers, one through bravery and fighting and her preferred one through cowardice.

Penance is the confession of sin, made with sorrow and with the intention of amendment, followed by penitential discipline. My penance, my sentence, was a lifetime under Stalin's rule. I refused it, and so karma made my life itself a sentence. I returned to Britain, after having cowardly left my sister behind. I soon married a woman who hated me and had a kid who hated me more. We eventually moved to the States, where I took a job driving a truck and dedicated my life to him. I invested my present and future into Karl Jr., *the visiting professor*. I was going to make up for my cowardly abandonment of my Dora by giving my life to this kid, my little Karl Jr.

The work seemed to have paid off, somewhat. While nobody in my family was smart, save for me and Dora, little Karl excelled academically. His mother was an acclaimed physician, who had published journal after journal. To this day, I cannot say if young Karl Jr. took more after Dora or his mother, only highlighting the fact that I do not even know my own son. I only knew that I loved this young, bright kid who grew to hate and reject me. Karma was not going to permit me to escape so easily from my sins associating with the German Nazis and cowardly leaving my little Dora to fend for herself behind the Iron Curtain. I eventually grew very sick. I even ended up unable to walk myself. Maybe fate was going to make feel the pain of the sister I had abandon to live out her life alone, under Communist rule.

After so many years, my wife left. I could not blame her. Who would stay with a man who did not even love her? I never even knew why I married her. I spent many nights on the dark, lonely roads pondering it and could only conclude that I used her company to fill a void that would never be filled. The woman I married had married me with unfair expectations. She was going to make up for my having left my sister behind in the depths of that gate. She was going to replace Anso and the child we had together, our only one, was going to replace your father, whom I had never met. I cannot blame young Karl Jr. for hating me. They always say the first child is the favored one, and I knew Karl Jr. was not my first. Every so often, I would check up on your father, unbeknownst to anybody. While I understood your grandfather's disdain for your father, it surprised me that the judge and the man I knew as the captain would treat a son that way, even if he knew it was not his. I always figured he worked to maintain this silly image of nobility that he believed came with his family name.

Old Man Frenz begins to laugh and cough simultaneously as he mentions "nobility and family name" and does not think this is coincidental.

The tense stillness of the air paralyze Josie and me. I always knew that my father was really the son of a German soldier whom my grandmother mentioned from time to time, but never during my grandfather's lifetime. However, I never knew that anyone else was aware, to include the German soldier himself. Now, here he is validating what I always knew but was not sure anyone else held such a malignant secret.

I take another hard swallow of my scotch. The irony.

We continue to drink on the porch as I continue to listen to Karl's stories. I had only heard about this odd fellow and am having a difficult time believing he is now here sitting here with me.

"I guess many people were adversely affected by the occurrences of the last century" is all I can come up with, as I lightly snuff out my cigar. Growing up American, we always have a rosy view of the world wars, a cherry-picked view that allows us to believe that good always wins out over evil. It only marginally occurs to us that those who help us pin down "the bad guys" are just as bad themselves, or even worse, and their victims would span decades.

"Well, you came here! You came to the States!" Josie interjects. "You see, the right side did win out. Freedom prevails. What my grandfather fought for was freedom."

Frenz chuckles, as he lights up another Camel. I wonder if his cigarette pack is a bottomless pit of filterless smokes.

"Oh yeah, you guys are free all right!" he says under his breath as he chuckles once more.

Through a camouflaging smokescreen of pot, cigarette, and cigar smoke, Josie shoots Karl a confused look.

"Americans love to think they are free! They love to brag about being the freest country in the world," Karl continues to chuckle, finally clueing in on Josie's inquisitive look.

"But how free are you? I have lived in many countries and have never seen people less free. The biggest tragedy of it is that Americans are people who make themselves the source of their own enslavement. Every so often, I see young Karl Jr's students. They are told from the earliest of ages that they have to attend the most expensive colleges; then when that pedigree is not sufficient, they dive further into debt. When they finally graduate, then they are told they have to settle down, buy a house, get married to someone they are most certainly to divorce, thus generating even more obligations." I can tell his rant has caught Josie's attention, as her avoidance of these traps, her true freedom, is scorned and branded her a misfit in a society that insists on partaking.

"Americans brag about their freedoms out of one corner of their mouth, but out of the other corner, tiptoe and dance on eggshells out of fear of offending the wrong group. Oh! How you people live in such fear!" I think of my mother, who always warned me about Facebook, in the terrified look in her eye when she warned me about it, as though any minute there would be a knock at the door.

I cannot help but to see how right this crude, sickly man is. How morbidly ironic that a little over a month before I am to lose the livelihood for which I toiled so hard for something I said online, I am now hearing this.

"Look how mercilessly you punish your own children. Again, I cannot count how many of my son's students were excelling academically and had the brightest of futures, whose lives are forever broken over marijuana! Ha! Pharmaceutical companies can sell you drugs that produce babies born with no arms, but someone barely a teenager will spend the rest of his life in prison as someone's sex slave for being caught with so many ounces of what amounts to a smelly plant!" At this point Karl is laughing, and I begin to laugh as well.

The laugh turned melancholy, though, as he continues.

"How many of your own veterans go to Afghanistan, come home with missing limbs, and for what? Now, if you make a video offending Muslims, and they claim that is what provoked their anger, you go to prison and not the violent offenders! Yes, you are so free here! And the ones returning without limbs probably don't have it as bad as the ones returning who cannot find jobs!"

His continued smoky-voiced dialogue begins to hit home. I am unemployed. I know fellow veterans who took their families and slept in their cars. I am being punished for something I said. As Old Man Frenz continue, I begin to think about the young kid I am supposed to prosecute and how helpless his parents seemed. He did not hurt anybody, he did not even do anything intentional, yet now he is fed to the lion's cage, or the ever-increasing gang and drug population.

"You know, my life was a tragic one! As I told you earlier, my life is my prison sentence. My life is my sentence, which is the *penance* that I must pay for my association with the Nazis, as good intentioned as it may have been. But as hideous as my life was, I do not envy you people! You take for granted all that was fought for, and you shamelessly give it away. Whores on New Year's Eve retain their dignities better than you guys!" And with that he crushes out his last Camel.

Surprise, I guess his cigarette pack is not limitless.

I find myself agreeing with completely.

"How ironic! The country forever reputed for its steadfastness virtue and bravery in the face of precarious darkness now rallies around cowards! You allow the weakest misfits of your society, those absentia any substance, character, or courage, to demand you not only recognize them but elevate them for barely doing a fraction of what most of you do." He continues to chuckle as much of a struggle as it seems. I can hear more of his labored wheezing as a result of emphysema.

"You are the only one who seems like he even half gets it!" he quips, "and I bet you are a recluse, aren't you?"

Damn! He is right! Does this guy see through me? Maybe he really does know that he is my grandfather.

"I'll have you know that my guest list is so extensive that I have to hire secretaries to manage my invitations. My top-floor condo suite is a round-the-clock affair, sir!"

"Yeah, right!" he chuckles. "I can tell by your mannerisms, you spend most of your time alone! I was the same way!"

He is right. Everything I do, from guitar, to writing, to running, is solitary. I traveled alone. I hate cruises but enjoy exploring new places. The dead voices of history come alive in the places I visit that offer me a solace, absentia the mindlessness concerns emitting from those around me. It drove my father crazy when I was a kid, but he was the same way. I knew why, but my father did not.

"And everyone thinks you have a bad attitude, don't they?"

My bad attitude and subsequent alcoholism stem from a disappointment with life in general. Growing up, I had a more than naive view of life in the US. We grew up believing that we were the arbiters of good in the world, and this was the land of opportunity. Today, jobs are scarce, if you can even find any. We were fed a lie, a lie that buried us in debt and misery. It takes this shriveled-up, offensive, old man, who once served in an army forever symbolic of all of mankind's depravity, to make me see. Such overwhelming disappointment sparks within me impatience in the company of the people with whom I am compelled to interact. Yet I would never admit this and am force-trained to concede that I am the one with mental difficulties. I was trained this way, in the same manner, a horse is trained by whip.

"Well, I do drink a lot. That is probably the impetus for my attitude," I reply.

"Drink a lot? Ha! You barely drink! Look, you have already slowed down!"

"Slowed down? Jesus! I *stopped*! It is nearly one in the morning!" I exclaim.

Frenz rolls his eyes and sighs as he shamelessly poured himself another.

"Yes, freedom! You guys fear everything! You worry about drinking too much and smoking too much. Yet your diets are hideous. You spend billions on psychotherapy. You have mass shootings almost weekly! Billions on nutritional supplements, yet you guys have the most heart attacks. You harp on about religion, family values, and you have a 60 percent divorce rate! It is incredible to watch, really; you have regulated yourself out of a life. I am not in tip-top shape, for certain, but I am nearly ninety! And after the life I have lived, I am damn ready to go!"

Karl Frenz represents everything for which American culture holds in disdain. He is old, while we spend millions on surgery to keep us young. He shamelessly drinks to excess, where we chide ourselves as binge drinkers for consuming more than six drinks weekly. He sucks down cigarettes, hates any unnecessary physical output, where we value and brag about our exercise. Most of all, Frenz, somewhat like my aunt, is going to live by his own law. Like me, he has been bought before and will not be bought again. His pride is gone, as he has borne the guilt of cowardly abandoning his sister. The only thing he has is himself and the freedom to be such. He is going to choose how to live and, more importantly, choose how to go out. As Frank Sinatra said, he is going to do it his way. I wonder if the people who so brag about their freedom should try to emulate.

The next day I am groggy, which only adds to the discomfort of the awkward day. The rest of the family stays back in the house as my grandmother wheels Old Man Frenz around the garden and to the tennis court my grandfather installed after he bought the house after the war.

"I can't believe this shit!" is the occasional phrase of disgust, accompanied by the occasional sigh, as we snack and sip our coffee in the covered porch that connects the kitchen and the rest of the house. They sit out there for what is the remainder of the afternoon. They hold each other's hands. Two people bonded by shared experiences, by shared struggles in caring for their family members. Two people bonded by catastrophic events, and ripped apart by those same catastrophic events. They continue to sit out there.

"Well, those of us that actually have something productive to do must get going!" Genny declares.

"Ditto that," Roselynn agrees.

Eventually, the rest of us, the cousins and their spouses, begin to be able to shift our attention from my grandmother to enjoying each other's company. Since we all went our separate ways over the last decade, we never had the opportunity to gather as we did when we were all in high school and college. No more Thanksgivings at Mamoun's house. Now here we all are, and we are silent. We start to slowly interact. Our parents, the siblings who did not storm off in disgust, are in the living room.

I wander in to pour another glass of wine. Basically, the only ones left just talking are my father and Dr. Karl Frenz Jr., the professor. I have to chuckle to myself.

"I must say! The last two people I would have ever imagined sitting in that living room talking would be my dad and the professor!" I announce to the porch, where my cousins grin at the irony. My father hates all media and distrusted them, and the professor, as he is known by his fans, is the worst one, as far as my father is concerned. Yet here they are, two men both rejected by their own fathers. Two men who should have grown up with the other father, now in the old, Victorian-styled living room where my father was forbidden to go as a kid, but where later, we had all of our family gatherings. It is not difficult to imagine that Judge Carlson would have loved the professor. They would have shared the same mannerisms, shared the same love of worship from those who considered themselves academic elites of intelligentsia. Meanwhile, after having spoken to Karl Frenz Sr. last night, who had up until last night been merely a dark secret of my grandmother's, could not have reminded me more of my own father.

Both my father and Old Man Frenz were truck drivers. They both shared the same rough mannerisms, the same attitudes. Frenz drove most of his routes through the north, Midwest, while my father did routes in the South. I wonder if they had ever before crossed paths. I wonder if they had ever sat across from each other at a random truck stop in the middle of an empty plain the Midwest, unaware that they were father and son.

Eventually, their time together ends, and my grandmother gives him a light kiss on the top of his head. She wheels him back to the house, where an impatient Karl Jr. and his handlers are anxiously awaiting to get back to the Tallahassee airport.

It is time for my grandmother and me to get to the task for which I even arrived in the first place. What was once a humble little farm that my grandfather had cheaply purchased to replace the serene paradise of the Benoit household for his new wife is now worth $10 million. Tallahassee had sprawled out and circled around it, choking out the peaceful farm with Publix shopping centers, gas stations, and Starbucks.

I watch as they load Old Man Karl on his custom-made van. He looks very sickly today. He has his oxygen mask, and his hands are shaking. Tears still stream out of his eyes. Once satisfied that his handlers properly loaded his father, Karl Jr. comes over to me. I hold out my hand, thinking he wants to shake it, but he does no such thing.

"Thank you, asshole, for getting my dad drunk last night! That was the last thing we needed on this useless, hellish trip we were forced to make!" And he spins around, not even waiting for my reply.

"Trust me!" I think to myself, "I think we all needed to get drunk!" I smile for the first time in months.

Seven

CLOSURE

C losure does not mean end. It is but the opening of another door. Closure is not only putting something to bed but putting something to be, for the purposes of transition, to something more.

Chief Justice Grey

I once delivered this message before sentencing a young man to life in prison without the possibility of parole. *My job is not easy, nor should it be envied. I sadly confess that throughout my life, my ambition to don the black robe was out of want for the power I thought it held. How stupid I was as a kid, and I cannot say I am any the wiser today. This is not a job of power but one of servitude, and that is the pain of it. I want to serve the people, but I know one family is going to walk out devastated by the judgment behind the slamming of this gavel. One family will walk out knowing their daughter's rape or their son's murder would receive no justice. One family will see their son be condemned to a life of imprisonment. Every morning, I wake up, shave, and know that someone's child is awaiting the death penalty on my orders. I do not say this to generate sympathy from yo, but only to highlight the brevity of what I must decide on a daily basis.*

I concluded by saying how that day's verdict and subsequent

sentencing was going to be easy. The man I was sentencing beat another man to a vegetative state over a football game. Unfortunately, days like that were rare. Most of the days, I hated reading the verdict and hated having to sentence. Over the years, the state assembly stepped in and made the sentencing easier as they mandated what crimes received what sentences.

Today I am chair of the board of ethics committee. This job is even worse. I cannot wait to retire. The pinnacle of my career was my long tenure as chief justice of the Georgia State Supreme Court. Overseeing the board of ethics is the fading twilight of it. If sentencing people bothered me, telling professionals they no longer have the licenses to practice their hard-earned professions kills me all the more. I have seen more than one grown man moved to tears after being denied the card for which he worked so hard, invested so much money, and passed one of the most rigorous exams.

Today will be one of those days. This will be one of the most painful ones, as the accused is the grandson of one of my heroes, one of my mentors, and a man who in all right is a civil rights icon himself. To add insult to injury, the accused is being called into question for the use of racial comments online, an irresponsible practice that no member of this fine profession should engage in. An officer of the court should exhibit behavior becoming of such.

I continue to pour through his comments. They are disgusting. He shares a YouTube video displaying a group of black youths pummeling a homeless veteran to death, followed by a subsequent comment. "Yep, and white privilege is the problem, folks!" I read another one of his posts, reads as follows: "black people have multiple kids with fifty different 'babies mommas' then let those kids get raised by gang rap, and then you want to blame the courts for being racist?? Please!"

The comments hit me personally; I was raised in a single-family household and have experience being a vet. When I came back from Vietnam, I was attacked by white people. When I returned from Vietnam, veterans were not thought fondly of. I myself was spit upon by antiwar protesters. Even more painfully, I was referred to as an "uncle Tom" and a "puppet of the white man's evil war" by one of my heroes, boxer Muhammed Ali! Many of those in the youth movement took their rage out on veterans, but being a black veteran was even worse. I was regarded not only as a baby killer but as a sellout to fight for a country and system that subjugated those of my race.

What they failed to understand was that this was not the America I saw. I understood well those black people who saw America as an oppressive place, where they were victimized and placed on the bottom of their society's ladder. I must admit, I myself felt this way more than enough. However, the America I saw was the one that Judge Victor Carlson had demonstrated to me.

My father was not so lucky. He came back from World War II. He jumped on the bus from Fort Dix and could not wait to travel home to see his wife and three-year-old son, whom he had never met. After twenty hours on the bus, it finally rolled through Thomasville, Georgia. His heart was thumping out of excitement.

"Sir, sir! This is my city!"

"Sit down, nigger! Bus stops in Tallahassee, and you can get off there!"

"Sir, that's thirty miles south of where I live."

"I said, sit down, nigger!"

I read Mr. Carlson's comments about black teens beating up a veteran, but I cannot help but to think of my father, dressed in his army uniform, adorned with medals, and still being called a nigger and told to sit down.

"This bus stops now!" another voice commanded.

Angrily, the bus driver looked up.

"If I have to stop this bus—"

"Have to stop?" the voice challenged. "You will stop this bus! And you will stop this bus now!"

The bus screeched to a slow but grinding halt. The driver hurriedly applied the last brake, and his massive frame struggled out of his seat, clearly flustered. Surprise replaced anger, as the driver saw confronting him a young major, with a limp shoulder, getting up to face him. Hesitantly, a few more soldiers stood up with him, and then a few more.

Major Carlson learned that day that if you take a stand, people will follow. I would like to think that moment is what propelled his civil rights career that inspired me to follow in the man's footsteps.

Many of those soldiers who stood with him did not like black people. Many of those soldiers could be heard throwing around racial slurs without so much as a thought. Yet they also realized that they had bled the same color, and wore the same color, and there was no such thing as a nigger when a man wore that uniform. This lesson that bus driver would never forget as he immediately stopped for my father.

"Thank you, sir!" my father said as he made his way toward the exit of the bus. He then looked back; Carlson was the guy with whom he would go on double dates with the French women in the Loire Valley, and also the surviving captain whose life he had saved in those dark, frigid Belgian forests.

My father must have been inspired as well by Carlson. For six days later, he confronted two men who called him a nigger, while he was in uniform collecting his benefits. He told them what Carlson had always said, about bleeding the same color, and wearing the same color. The men did not buy it, and that night five more people and beat him to death. My father, who fought with the Buffalo Soldiers in the Battle of the Bulge, a battle that was final defeat to Adolf Hitler and his evil regime, was lynched in his own hometown.

I grew up without a father and wince whenever I hear people on talk radio talk about "the black family" or talk about "fatherless families" as if they have any idea. To read Carlson's grandson's comments breaks my heart. His grandfather knew too damn well and understood too well how easy it was for a black man in the fifties to end up in jail.

Nevertheless, I am going to give him a chance. I pulled him in my office and laid out what he needed to do. I think if I give him a chance, he can still be the man his grandfather was. I knew his grandfather well. I watched him argue in court, then watched him on the bench. Later, when I passed the bar and started a family of my own, I would invite him and his family to come to church with us. Living in the times I did, and knowing the fate of my father, I lived in fear. My belief in Christ freed me from this fear. I grew up knowing that if Christ could fearlessly take the cross and scorn of the Romans who place him there, then I could face those who would lynch me or give me the same fate as my father. In over fifty-five years, I am proud to say I have missed very few services. I invited Judge Carlson, and he came alone, as he explained his wife did not attend church. I had met Miss Anne Sophie many times. She was a pleasant but stubborn woman. Please, young Carlson, be the man your grandfather was.

———— ((●)) ————

I look at the diploma on my wall. It reads *Shannon Chevalier Carlson*. I remember earning that diploma from John Marshall, and later being sworn in as an officer of the court, and member of the State Bar of Georgia.

Today is my hearing. I am prepared to humble myself and apologize in front of the whole forum. I am prepared, but I am really not. I wince at the thought of having to grovel to this board. I was taunted, bullied, by a guy who lays down the most racially charged, offensive online comments with absent thought impunity. Yet I say one thing back to him, and now I have to script an entire monologue of reconciliation, highlighting painful details of some supposed disorder, clearly a result of *my privilege*. I then must convince these arbiters that although I am naturally tainted, I am able to be cured, willing to do what I must to exact such a cure, and worthy of the opportunity to be cured.

I will sit in front of a board of seven judgmental attorneys and bare it all. Now I realize how strippers feel, baring everything, including their dignity, in front of nonappreciative losers, just to maintain a livelihood. Few onlookers will be there, some will be waiting to have their case heard, some people just have no lives, I suppose. I have seen a few of these, and they are rarely pleasant.

I do not want to go. I waited until the last minute to leave, a risky venture, given the traffic here. It took all the discipline of a Buddhist monk to make myself get up the stairs into that building. This is unfair. Why am I the only one accountable for what I say? Why are the people who cruelly mock my situation, why do they get to say what they want, and I am held to account?

"So, Mr. Carlson. We are convened here today in complaint of online comments you had made on Facebook and Twitter. We are responding to complaints of racism and discriminatory behavior. Sir, your response?"

I try to swallow, but my throat is too dry. My desperate gulp only catches air, which worsens my scratchy throat.

I know that I have to apologize but cannot bring myself to do it.

"Sir, I have nothing to say," I reply meekly. I feel the widened eyes gaze upon me and loo up to see the chief justice's narrowing gaze upon me.

"I am sorry, but I have done nothing wrong."

One of the board members, Miss Adelson, pipes up.

"Mr. Carlson, we feel that your online behavior exhibits—"

I immediately interrupt.

"Right! I exhibited. That is what I did. I exhibited a behavior, but it was only an exhibition, an expression. Nobody was lynched as a result of what I typed online." I see the chief justice wince at my mention of the word *lynch*.

"Nothing I uttered sparked a riot. I have never hurt anybody, I have not stolen from anybody, I have not made any misrepresentations on which another party relied to their financial detriment or ruin. I am here because somebody claims they were hurt by my words. Somebody, I might add, who was using his words to hurt me. Yes! Somebody who hurled hurtful words my way, in a direct attempt to ridicule, degrade, and celebrate what has been a hellish ordeal for me, had equally hateful words hurled back at him, and he did not like it. I am here because I supposedly hurt the feelings of someone who I truly do not believe was hurt by my words but in fact is here in this room grinning and is simply using this procedure as a smokescreen with which to attempt to ruin me."

"Mr. Carlson!" the chief justice interrupts in his thunderous voice, but I ignore him and continue.

"No difference exists between mocking a person's pitiful state and mocking someone's race, except we have made race a forbidden topic. But I would argue that each are equally hurtful, maybe the economic scenario more so, as it is more personal than a person's ethnicity, which is more culture based, and one may choose to act in conformity or defiance to the culture to which they were raised. Basically, the guy who offended me has a race card, and I have no such luxury. I have no racial protections I can pull out as a handy defense to hurtful words thrown my way. I have to endure his mockery, and he has this board."

"Mr. Carlson, I am rapidly tiring of your mischaracterization of this board!" the chief justice again thunders. "This board is not a smokescreen, as you so casually and mockingly put it, but a committee of the most accomplished officers of the court, as well as jurists such as myself to ensure all ethical complaints are addressed and solved in a judicious and expedient manner. Its purpose is to uphold the respect and integrity of this noble profession."

I stop and wait. I take a breath. Saliva returns to my mouth I begin to feel alive again.

"Yes, Chief Justice, I realize how much this committee means to you, sir. Which is why I feel compelled to appeal to your better judgment and see this complaint and its subsequent hearing for what it is, a personal vendetta."

"Mr. Carlson! How dare you question my judgment! I will have you know I have had cases before me that far exceeded the little teenage kid case that broke you down, sir! And I will not have you subjugate the integrity of these proceedings. More than one person came forward, offended and disturbed by your online behavior. Now, because you are a member of the bar, we, as the honor guards of the state bar, voted and felt compelled to formally address this matter!

"Now, I advised you on what you needed to do, and you come in here mocking this board, this procedure, and carrying on in a combative posture! Now I want to know, what do you think your grandfather would say if he were here!"

My grandfather—he means Judge Carlson, but I wonder what Old Man Frenz would say.

"My grandfather! Yes, of course! My grandfather! I have spent my life being compared to him. The majority of my youth was spent living his idealistic vision. I wanted nothing more than to follow precisely in his footsteps. "

"Then what changed?" The chief justice asks forcefully but inquisitively.

"I served in the military. I then decided to attend law school, out of sincere belief of the Constitution I had once swore to defend. Now I stand here, penalized for something I printed online."

"Mr. Carlson, you know that the First Amendment—" starts one of the board members.

"Yes, I understand," I reply. "I know the First Amendment protects you from criminal prosecution and does not absolve one of personal responsibility for anything they say or private parties they may offend. But you are missing the point. You guys are here to make me apologize for something I said or deprive me of my livelihood. You are an ethics committee. Your job is to ensure and enforce ethical behavior."

"And, sir, do you believe that your behavior online is ethical?"

"What I did may not be moral, but I have breached zero ethics standards."

"And how do you figure this does not encroach on your ethical standards whatsoever? Do you think making public racist statements qualifies as ethical behavior?" another member peppers at me.

"What I did may not be moral. But it damn sure isn't unethical."

"Your language, Mr. Carlson! And please enlighten me as to what you think the difference is!" the chief justice presses.

"What constitutes moral is within the eye of the beholder and differs according to one's personal values. Ethics is more concrete. Ethics is not using one's superior position to disadvantage another to their own enrichment. Ethics is not using one's superior knowledge to disadvantage another. A doctor making a false diagnosis to a patient in order to milk the patient's insurance is unethical. He is using his superior knowledge to his own advantage and to the disadvantage of another. An attorney who starts a business with a layperson unskilled in business and tells the business partner to give him all intellectual property rights is unethical. But morals are completely subjective. One may think purchasing pornography is immoral, one may think consuming alcohol is immoral. But so long as you are not disadvantaging people, it is never unethical. Unethical behavior is always immoral also, but *only sometimes* can behavior considered immoral be unethical."

"Well sir, we thank for that very enlightening lesson on ethics," pipes the Chief Justice, in his deep booming voice.

"You seem to have a good grip on ethics," another voice says.

"Perhaps! I think the fact that I have to lay this out for you is sad. I think the fact that you are making me answer for something that I really—"

"For making racists statements!" the chief justice interrupts.

"Online public racist statements! And, might I add, public racist statements that, uttered by an officer of the court and member of this state bar, reflect poorly on the entire profession to include everyone sitting here! You seem to not understand that your comments as a member of the bar may be attributed to any member of that bar. If you want to embarrass yourself in public with your drunken comments, that is definitely your choice! But I will be goddamned if I let your behavior tarnish the sterling reputation of these accomplished people here and every other advocate of people's rights and remedies by your grotesque, antiquated, offensive comments!" he thunders, visibly irritated. I never thought that I would hear a very outwardly churchgoing and faith-driven chief justice take the name of God in vain and never think that I will if I live another hundred years, a testament to how angry he was growing.

"Again, offensive, but not unethical. You are the board of ethics and not the board of civility. And let me be honest—each one of you on this board has acted, let's just say, less than civil at some point in your lives! One of you on this board sentenced a kid to twenty years for violating probation!"

"Mr. Carlson, I believe I have heard enough!" He regains his reputed calm demeanor and sighs. "I appreciate your self-righteous, patriotic, 'pity me' lecture on your view of ethics. But we have wasted enough of these people's time! Now, last month, I did you the courtesy of advising you what you needed to do to get back in the good graces of the bar. Are you prepared to do that today? Because to be very honest with you, I am rapidly tiring of your antics!"

"You mean apologize, Mr. Chief Justice?"

"Are you prepared to do that?"

I pause. My dry throat is now on fire. I try so hard to push down a swallow, to prevent the well pressuring behind my eyes. I cannot break down and cry in front of these people. But I am becoming more and more distressed. Am I really going to do this? Am I really going to relinquish a livelihood I have always dreamed of obtaining but thought beyond my intellectual capacity? I can look into the future and see my mother's disgusted face. Now my family will really think I am a loser, and none of them are with me here today.

I feel truly alone. I am here to face these people on my own. No moral support, no "I love you," "you will do fine," no "do what you think is right."

Perhaps it is not too late to apologize, but I cannot make myself do it. I cannot bring myself to grovel. I just cannot stomach it. I have to beg these people's forgiveness for talking back to someone online. I have to beg forgiveness for an opinion, as offensive and unkind as it is. I take a sniff, in lieu of being able to swallow. My vision begins to blur with tears.

"Are you sure you do not want to reconsider your position there, son? You are looking upset." The chief justice probes.

I so badly want to be strong. I think of my grandmother, and the story she told me. I remember how she told me she walked into a tabac that had been forbidden by German forces that had taken over her city. She told the story of how flustered she was. How badly she wanted to assert herself, but like myself, she knew she was overwhelmed in force and outpowered, and she knew she was powerless and just teared up in front of the soldier.

I heard my grandmother's story numerous times. Now, I know how she felt firsthand. Here I was trying desperately to hold my own and stick to my guns in front of these imposing, judging figures. Although we are colleagues, I know none of them regard me as their equal, but an inferior whose obligation it should be to cower in front of them. And here I am, ready to break down, cry and display to them that they have in fact broken me. They will have succeeded. I will cower and come undone in front of them, just as my grandmother did in front of an imposing young Corporal Frenz. Frenz. I don't know what makes me think of him.

Something makes me look back. I do not know what it was, but before I completely break down, I look back. I see one last time the mocking glare of the guy at whom I aimed my slur. He has a victorious look mixed with one of surprise that I can draw out the conflict to such a losing conclusion, and surprisingly, even a hint of respect that I am willing to actually stand up and fight as opposed to proffer some wimpy, half-hearted apology.

Then I see him! There he is among the slovenly, entertained onlookers, the old man in a wheelchair. Of all the people hanging out in the back, watching this monstrosity, there *he* is. While everyone else is shaking their heads, some laughing at my visibly shaken and defeated self, Old Man Karl Frenz nods his head at me. A man who knows what it is to grovel, knows what it is to be punished for what he says, came here to see if I would do the same.

My eyes dry up a little. I reassert myself and politely tell them what they do not expect to hear.

"Your Honor, sir, I do not think at this point, I am ready to apologize. I am not ready to apologize to this idiot or this board! I am still resolute in the fact that I did nothing wrong. What I said may have hurt some people, but I should not be made to apologize."

The minute I push those words up through my diaphragm and now stone-dry throat, I feel my stomach instantly sink. I stand there not knowing what is holding my trembling legs afoot.

"Very well, Mr. Carlson. You leave us no choice. We will take a quick recess to confer among ourselves and reconvene in ten minutes." the chief justice commands. "In the meantime, you will remain here."

The door opens behind me, and I look around to just see the old man wheel himself out. I want so badly to chase after him. They tell me I am to remain, but they are disbarring me anyway, so who cares. I guess deep down I care. I remain there in my seat, waiting for my sentence.

I keep hoping that any minute those assholes on the board will reappear, hurry, and end this nonsense, ruin my life, so that I can bolt out of the door and catch up with Old Man Frenz. My impatience only seems to make the time pass that much slower. As cruel as it may have sounded, I am counting on and eagerly hoping that Frenz's condition will cause him to move slowly, permitting me time to bolt out of there and chase after him. He is the only one I have by my side. When everyone else had thrown up their hands, he came to at least show solidarity. Finally, someone believes that I am not the disgraceful monster everyone else who gathered here thinks me to be.

Finally, the door opens. The committee streams out and takes their time arranging themselves and taking their seats at the board. I wonder if it is only me, or do people sense when one is in a hurry and purposely drag on? Once they are seated, they take another few slow, agonizing minutes speaking coarsely among themselves and then clearing their throats.

Finally, the chief justice speaks up. I nervously look around. Some people have a look of grave concern from the spectacle that just saw unfold in my exchange with the chief justice. The jerk who reported me in the first place is still there grinning and shaking his head, a gleam of respect in his eyes that I had not yet registered, and never would.

"Mr. Carlson, after convening for a few minutes, the board has reached a conclusion." He pauses and glares up at me, briefly, glancing over the rim of his glasses, "Mr. Carlson, it is our recommendation that your license be suspended for a time indefinite and to be later determined by this board."

And there are the words that strike through and hollow me! My knees go numb and have no idea what is holding me up.

"The board of the ethics committee has concluded that you not only present a poor representation of what an officer of the court and member of the bar should represent but you show zero remorse in the pain your words inflict on your fellow colleagues..."

He continues on, but as the shock of what I knew was the inevitable wore off, he may as well have been reading me an obscure poem, for my mind is preoccupied with scurrying out the door and catching the old man. It never fails. Whether it was a briefing in the military that ran over, when I was already late for a date, or a court case that went well into the evening, when I had concert tickets, time knew when I needed it, and like most people in my life, that was when it eluded me.

As stubborn as time could be, even *it* must end, and recompose elsewhere. Finally, the chief justice concludes.

"Good luck to you, sir, and may God bless you!" he pauses, looks up, pain in his eyes, "While you may find this difficult to believe, we do wish for the best of you son!" he called me *son*.

He grimaces as he says those last words. He utters the last words in pain and discomfort. I think disbarring me bothers him more than me. All I want to do is get the hell out of there. I want to catch up with my grandfather, a man who until recently was merely a dark secret in my grandmother's life.

When I finally make it outside the building, Old Man Frenz is being loaded on his van. I want to run after him. I want to talk more with him. Perhaps the realization that I finally met this man, whom I had not even known or heard of until only a few years ago, and even then, he was but a long-ago story, has yet to sink in. I want to spend a little more time with him, beyond simply our late-evening cocktail-and-weed session.

While watching Karl Jr, on CNN, he announces that his father has died. He is very curt about it and goes through the bullet points of his father's history, as though he were lecturing one of his old students, *German army, British citizen, and truck driver*. The old, broken-down man who put a distant son through school, who drove a rig through a cold New England evening so that his son could afford Ivy League schools, gets only the briefest of mentions. Dignitaries, former ambassadors, former four-star admirals, now working as consultants, and UN officials are often repeat guests who take minutes upon minutes of the professor's hourlong show, but not his father. My bitterness at the visiting professor, whose show I used to enjoy so much, will never subside for his lack of respect for my grandfather!

Not too long after the professor announced that his father passed, the day I never wanted to think about came to be. I got a call from my mother saying that Mamoun had passed peacefully in her sleep. Frenz and my grandmother represented two different outcomes of a time that transformed the world, and with their passing, the last remnants of a generation went with them.

Closure is not simply closing the book on something but the transition to something else. I do not know where Old Man Frenz is, but I know with his life here, he transitioned to something much more profound. Meanwhile, I transition to a job as a home-based travel agent. I am not sure how many home-based travel agents there are who hold juris doctorates in this country, but they must be the happiest souls in the world.

I used to spend my day talking about years behind bars, unleashed into a jungle confined within a concrete block. I used to spend my day listening to horror stories from the inside.

Then I spend my day telling people about the cheapest way to visit Cape Town, South Africa. I tell them that the hostels there are as nice as hotels here, but only forty bucks a night. Long have I been a fan of irony. I was removed from a profession that was killing me for my conduct online, and now I have a job that enlivens me by talking to people online. I tell them when they visit Waikiki, Hawai'i, they can stay on Kunio, instead of on Kalakakaua, and it cuts their hotel fare by 60 percent.

Once I earn enough money, I decide to coup my savings and move down to Montanita, Ecuador, a small enclave of a surf town on the Pacific coast of South America, a quick three hours north of the capitol, Guayaquil. In addition to booking online trips, I now run a daquiri stand, where I serve drinks to English, German, and American expats and tourists who dare to brave the shores and culture of Ecuador. I live in a shack on a two-acre farm up the street. Each day I awaken to my homegrown marijuana and then proceed to pick fresh oranges, bananas, and pineapples, throw them in a basket, and bike down the hill to the coast, where I will mix fresh drinks and hope I do not get too drunk myself. American and Euro tourists greet me as I mix for them their crude dichotomic concoction of vitamin-enriched natural fruit and body-killing ethanol.

It is completely free here, and I honestly would not want to be anywhere else. On second thought, Cape Town, South Africa, would not be bad, nor would Fiji, but this is as close to perfect as I could ever hope for. I wonder how different Michael's life would have been if his parents had merely taken the six hundred dollars to fly him down here, instead of standing trial for something so ridiculous as to be embarrassing. Instead of being a legal concubine slave to the nation's scum, he could have built a carefree life here, thousands of miles safe from our country's encroaching jurisdiction. It took my meeting with Karl Frenz to realize how truly free I was not, but how free I could become. Irony, receiving a lesson in freedom from a former soldier of a regime infamous for its very antithesis.

I received a letter from the board reinstating my law license. My parents sent it to me, as the address was forwarded to them. It is nice to have my card back, but I have closed the book. Closure is not really the end of something, but the transition, and I love how this closed.

CPSIA information can be obtained
at www.ICGtesting.com
Printed in the USA
LVHW031508240821
695994LV00005B/172

9 781977 228307